Almost Single

Almost Single

Advaita Kala

A Bantam Discovery

ALMOST SINGLE
A Bantam Discovery Book
First published in India in 2007 by HarperCollins Publisher India
Bantam Discovery trade paperback / March 2009

Published by Bantam Dell
A Division of Random House, Inc.
New York, New York

Book design by Carol Malcolm Russo

Bantam Books and the rooster colophon are registered trademarks and
Bantam Discovery is a trademark of Random House, Inc.

Library of Congress Cataloging-in-Publication Data
Advaita Kala.
Almost single / Advaita Kala. — Bantam discovery trade pbk.
p.   cm.
ISBN 978-0-553-38610-3 (trade pbk.)
1. Women—India—Fiction.   2. Mothers and daughters—Fiction.
3. Mate selection—Fiction.   4. India—Social life and customs—
Fiction.   5. Domestic fiction.   I. Title.

PR9499.4.A344A79 2009
823'.92—dc22
2008042602

Printed in the United States of America
Published simultaneously in Canada

www.bantamdell.com

BVG 10 9 8 7 6 5 4 3 2 1

To Girvani and Devanshu Dhyani,
to the beginnings that await you
and the joy you bring each other

"Would you tell me, please, which way I
ought to go from here?"
"That depends a good deal on where you
want to get to," said the Cat.
"I don't much care where—," said Alice.
"Then it doesn't matter which way you go,"
said the Cat.
"—so long as I get *somewhere,*" Alice added as
an explanation.
"Oh, you're sure to do that," said the Cat, "if
you only walk long enough."

—Lewis Carroll,
  Alice's Adventures in Wonderland

My World

*T*he phone punctures my deep dreamless REM slumber at the crack of dawn. I flop an arm out of the covers, groping for the instrument. "Hello," I croak.

"Aisha, wake up, sleepyhead." Misha sounds like a bottle of the best bubbly ready to pop, and my head feels like it's going to explode. *Just what happened last night?*

"What time is it?"

"Quarter to eleven o'clock, and it's a gorgeous day! Do you want to get a coffee at Barista? We can sit outside."

I hang up.

Of course it rings again. Damn, some women just don't get it.

"Yes, Mish," I grind out. "No coffee for me, it stains the teeth."

"Come on! You smoke like a pack a day. Don't give me that."

I refuse to dignify this with a response. But knowing there is no point in arguing, I agree to meet her at eleven-thirty, which gives me forty-five minutes more of shut-eye. I lie back in bed, bracing myself for the wave of nausea that I can feel making its way up my throat. It is broken by a flurry of recollection.

Last night was girls' night out. Let me rephrase that: *Most* nights are girls' night out. The only difference is that last night we stayed in. Misha had invested in a bottle of plonk with some French-sounding label. In consideration of the money spent, we finished the bottle, for which I was paying the full price now.

For most people, life and love are like a game of connect-the-dots: The numbers always form a straight line to the goal. The result is a perfect picture. For the lesser half—especially for those who inhabit my world—the vision is a blur of blots and splotches and there's no straight line to speak of.

This is my story, and of those who occupy this world with me. My name is Aisha Bhatia, I am twenty-nine years old and single. But before I get into all that, I have a confession to make: I am rather large. I live in denial, of course, and will never tell you how much I weigh. Let's just say that the package isn't too bad as my height sort of makes up for my generous proportions. Maybe this sounds too much like an Alcoholics Anonymous introduction, but I don't know what else to say. I hate my job—actually, my boss—so I don't want to get into that. I don't really care for my vital stats at the moment, and I don't have a cute/funny nickname either. Hence this introduction. It stinks, but it sticks. Actually, it's quite in sync with the way society looks upon single women of a certain age. In fact, sometimes I think there should be support groups like AA out there for us. If I ever do quit my job, I'll start one.

Did I say single? Well, I do have one "serious" ex-boyfriend. We are now "friends" and the split was "amicable." So why the inverted commas? Because breakups are always tricky. I believe I am going through this love renaissance thingy, which involves reexamining my relationships and social bonds. In all honesty, we are in touch because he is my bitch fix when I have it in for the world, and in particular for the male species. Like, when shrinks tell you that all your adult problems can be traced back to your childhood? My own psychoanalysis tells me that all my present romantic hiccups can be traced back to the ex.

I have two friends, Misha and Anushka—soul buddies, really—and their opinions pretty much dictate my life. When I'm not busy psychoanalyzing them, myself, others, or the world in general, I work in a hotel and lead a very busy life, meeting a lot of interesting people along the way. Yes, I'm being facetious here. People who spend upward of ten grand a night on a bed can be a pain. Though not as much as the sorry man who calls himself my boss—but more on him later. So, in brief, I tolerate my job, hate my boss, annoy my ex, and bond big time with my friends, while routinely suffering from umbilical-cord whiplash thanks to my mother. All this while living under the open sky of the urban, second-fastest-growing-economy-in-the-world, India.

And just what do I do at the hotel? Sometimes I have to ask myself that question. Is this what it means to have a calling, a purpose? I work as a guest relations manager at the Grand Orchid Hotel. I dine at five-star restaurants, stay at five-star luxury hotels during my travels, can name old- and new-world wines with great élan, and can tell my cheeses apart. That's the calling, and I've found a way of fitting it to a T. Except the T now stands for tedious and tiresome. The hours suck and the salary does not reflect the rates we charge.

Anyway, back to the events of last night. It was as we drank the last of the wine that Misha brought up the subject of desivivaha.com. Yup, you've guessed it, Misha is on the wrong side of twenty-nine as well. She knows this person at work whose cousin was sailing in our raft until as recently as last week. (I say "raft" because a boat would be too large for what is, tragically, a small minority; not too many women in India are over twenty-nine and single, with jobs, not careers, which means the "she's-really-career-focused" stuff doesn't stick either.)

Anyhow, desivivaha.com came to the rescue of this twenty-nine-plus coz and saved her from the dingy raft—also, of course, eating into the rapidly depleting reserve of single and eligible men over thirty. And now, Misha informed me, there she was, all thanks to desivivaha.com, happily married, dusting rooms, and cooking up a storm of desi (Indian) food in the windy city of Chicago.

Did I mention that Misha's one and only ambition is to net the perfect NRI—non-resident Indian? It is in pursuit of this goal that she moved from Bhatinda to New Delhi. And now she's decided it's a grand idea to register with desivivaha.com—the one-stop site for an NRI to hold tight. So we logged on and spent the next forty-five minutes thinking up glowing adjectives to describe our assets and ambivalent ones to dodge the iffy bits.

"Hike up your annual income by a couple of lakhs, it'll keep the broke types away," Misha suggested. So I fudged my salary, and then I fudged my weight and body type. The fudging was addictive, like a drug you couldn't get enough of, though bags of potato chips are more my thing than high-end hallucinogenics.

Just as I hesitantly set about posting my glamorously enhanced stats on the net, divine intervention arrived in the form of the absence of my photograph. Misha, however, found a fabulous photograph of herself except for one small detail—her ex-boyfriend was in it. A word of advice to those looking at this Internet option: A photograph multiplies your chances of netting a mate exponentially.

So we scanned the picture, opened Photoshop, and managed to expunge him from it. Five minutes later we had a pic to die for, except that Misha had a strange arm in black snaking over her bare shoulders. I assured her that one couldn't really tell as it was an evening shot. I knew the bare-shoulder look was a bit bold, but when an Indian girl of marriageable age eschews domestication by pretending that she can't tell her daals (lentils) apart, desperate measures are called for.

So, as of this morning, we are both officially registered on desivivaha.com and the man of our dreams is just a click away.

I groan as I lie in bed thinking of the intimate— and deeply exaggerated—details of my life plastered all over the World Wide Web. I know without an iota of doubt that it is going to cost me dearly.

I make it to the loo and stand under the hot shower until my skin begins to resemble a wrinkled old prune, probably the kind used to make the horrible wine we had last night. As I pull on my faithful pair of track pants and a tee, I unwittingly catch a glimpse of myself in the full-length mirror. Fresh as a five-day-old daisy in a water-deprived vase. But people who have a higher purpose in life don't let a little vanity hold them back. I open the door and gingerly climb down the stairs, then set off for the neighborhood Barista.

Misha, the pint-size dynamo, sits perched on a quaint cane chair, under a huge parasol, in oversize sunglasses and a cloud of Eternity. I shield my eyes with my arm to cut the glare.

"I thought it was a gorgeous day," I remark snidely.

"One can never be too careful with the sun," Misha replies, zenlike. Cleansing, toning, and moisturizing are her three steps to Nirvana. I order a double espresso and sit back, squinting in an effort to brave the sun and her radiance. Misha is all of five feet and really cute in a guys-just-want-to-protect-her kind of way. Her hair is cut in a feathered French crop, and she has gorgeous dimples and twinkling eyes. She looks rather like an overfed cherub since she has put on weight lately and her clothes are bursting at the seams. Of course, I would never point that out to her. She gives me the brightest of smiles.

"Okay, about last night's website thingy," she begins. This is what I love about girlfriends. Unlike with guys, when you have to enact a whole screenplay before you broach a topic, with girls you can just read one another's minds. "Have you got a response?"

But this time we are clearly not on the same page. "When did we register? Like five hours ago? Come on, how can they respond so soon?"

"Aisha, it was daytime in America, and London is a good five hours behind. Be realistic!"

"Right, I forgot the target group. So, how do these potential husbands respond?"

"To your email address, silly. I put your work one down. You do have remote access, right?"

"My work mail? Are you crazy!" Vivid thoughts of my oily, rotund boss accessing my email flash through my mind. Recently, an ex-colleague was caught emailing our standard operating procedures to a competitor, so now all email accounts are subjected to random checks. Though it is not standard operating procedure, our boss does it regularly just to keep himself busy. Now he will be privy to my inner desperation. The hotel grapevine will be abuzz with my online shopping for a husband! "Misha, you have to get me off this thing. It was a drunken mistake!"

Misha shoots me a wounded look that becomes one of determination. "No, Aisha, we have to take being single into our own hands. There is a whole world of men out there and we have to reach them! This is the way to do it! We are too cosmopolitan for the local boys, we have to expand our horizons and harness the benefits of technology. . . ."

She is getting onto her soapbox and needs to be knocked down a peg or two. But I can never bring myself to be the one to do it. "Okay, okay! Just get my work email off it, all right? And don't talk so loudly. We don't want the whole world to know we are doing this."

Misha gives me a triumphant smile. "Fine. I'll direct the emails to my account. Just remember that fortune favors the brave."

"Yup, and men can smell a desperate woman a mile away."

———

Two double espressos later, I am back home and, unsurprisingly, fall asleep again. I guess a monumental hangover followed by a caffeine overdose can be a bit much. It is a waste of a Sunday, but I am too tired to care. I wake up at six in the evening, starving and desperate for something greasy. I order a pizza and reach for the TV remote. I idly channel-surf, pausing at a shot of a smoky nightclub. Whenever they have a shot of a smoky nightclub on a Hindi news channel, you can be sure that it's reportage with a slant on sleaze. The story invariably revolves around illicit sex or drugs when it's a "scoop" and both when it's "breaking news." And the captions almost always include words like *ashleel* and *jalwa*. (Thanks to these channels, my Hindi vocab has improved dramatically, although mostly with words I wouldn't use in polite company.)

I watch long enough to spot Ric, a former classmate of mine, lolling his head from side to side with a cigarette in his mouth. The camera pans the crowd again and settles on another dude doing some similarly cool moves. Nic, another good friend. Then and there I am hit by a watershed moment. I realize there is no getting away from the fact that time is running out. And my life is awful. I have a job that sucks, I have not had a steady relationship in years, and my bank balance is...well, let's not even go there. I really don't know where I am headed, and yes, I am a smoker. It must be the subject of the program that triggered the moment: *Heart Ailments*. Suddenly, my peer group is the subject of a demographic study.

I feel the onset of an anxiety attack and then, in a telepathic twist, the phone rings. It is my mother. "I hope you aren't spending time with *those* boys, they are just trouble." She launches an attack on my friends without preamble.

What are the chances that in today's age of a gazillion programs, you and your mother happen to be watching the same channel? I mean, hello, isn't one of those soap opera K-serials on?

"Come on, Ma, just 'cuz they are on this silly news clip doesn't mean they are trouble," I say, defending Nic and Ric.

"Are they married yet?" Mama Bhatia can sort through and file people on the basis of their marital status with the speed of a Pentium 4 processor.

"No, Ma, not as yet." I smile to myself, thinking how horrified Nic and Ric would be at the mere mention of marriage.

"Well, it's all very well for them, they are boys and it's okay if they marry late. Don't let that influence you. They don't have to bear children and all. Although which sensible family would give their girls to those two?"

Well, plenty actually. The older a guy gets, the bigger his dating pool. It works just the reverse for women. We come attached with a "best before" tag, and if—God forbid!—we reach the expiration date while still single, it's downhill all the way from there.

The finest and most honest indicator of one's market value, I've discovered, is the street urchin or peddler. Here's how it works: You start out being called *baby* and then the respectful *didi,* then comes the biggest and most traumatic transition, from *didi* to the dreaded *aunty;* and finally, the truly godawful *mataji.* But in today's Botoxed world, if you get to the *mataji* stage, you probably don't care anyway. I've been called *aunty* on some rare occasions, but mostly *didi,* so I figure I'm still good to go.

"So, have you met anyone interesting?" My mother raises her favorite subject.

I am surprised at the time it has taken for her to bring it up. Usually I answer the phone and like a bullet that had already left the cylinder, it is the first thing shot at me. If I ever do get married, I wonder how she will start a conversation with me.

"Well, no one between yesterday and today, but there's always tomorrow."

"Don't be sarcastic with your mother. She only asks because she cares about you." When my mother speaks about herself in the third person, she is *very* upset. I quickly apologize. "Anyway, Deepak is getting married," my mother announces.

Deepak is the neighborhood catch. God has been economical in the looks and personality departments, but generous with the cash. Every aunty worth her salt with an eligible daughter in tow has been eyeing him since puberty. It's like the gong went off in the ghanta ghar—the clock tower—the day he sprouted his first facial hair, announcing his availability to everyone.

"He is? Does he still look like...?" I begin uncharitably.

"Beta, when it comes to boys like that, who looks

at the face," my mother answers wisely. Money does conquer all. Someone should update the old adage.

"Well, good for him," I reply disinterestedly.

"Everyone is getting married now. Chalo, it's all karma at the end of the day."

My mother hangs up and I stare at the receiver in dismay.

When your parents stop matchmaking and turn philosophical it's time to worry.

I pick up my phone and speed-dial. No, I don't have a groom on standby. I am calling my astrologer. Nothing is more indicative of my belief in him than the number one status he enjoys on my speed-dial. I am a traditionalist in that sense. I know it's trendy to go to tarot-card readers, but Shastriji is very accurate, and he is the family astrologer. Most important, he keeps my secrets. "Shastriji, *namaste, aap kaise hain?*"

"*Theek hoon*. How are you?"

"I am fine also. I need to ask you something." I state the obvious.

"*Haan, bolo?*"

"Do you see marriage in my future?"

"Well, your stars are changing. Lagna yog starts on the twenty-first of this month. This time is very auspicious for marital alliances." Shastriji is a computer whiz; he has it all on his PC.

"So do you see me getting married soon?" I ask, getting straight to the point.

"Ummm . . . The time is auspicious. . . . So let's see . . . there are indications."

Shastriji is also the Artful Dodger; he never commits to anything. I think that's what keeps me going back. I can never say for certain that he was wrong about something.

There are always "indications."

The Second Sherwani Guys

*S*ometimes I have these vivid fantasies about entering the Grand Orchid from the front gate, as opposed to the service entrance that we menials are beholden to use. I picture a grand cavalcade of vintage motor vehicles beginning its ascent at the base of the two-hundred-meter ramp. My rickety old Fiat Padmini, on the other hand, takes a little longer to huff up the circuitous ramp that has been designed to mimic the access to a well-guarded fort.

The driveway of the Grand Orchid is flanked by large trees that provide natural shelter to the line of fancy cars constantly parked along the sides. Hotel valets are seriously discerning when it comes to choosing parking spots for these vehicles. If your car is of some significance, it will be parked right in the front. If it's a vehicle of more humble origins, you can be assured that on a busy night, getting to your car will be as challenging as navigating the Arabian Sea in a rowboat.

The majestic trees relinquish their embrace to reveal a monument in white. Some say the building is reminiscent of the Raffles Hotel in Singapore. I don't know about that, but it does have its origins in the East or, rather, in yesteryear Siam. It seems that a wealthy nawab from some obscure state in central India, while on a visit to Siam, fell in love with a local beauty and duly brought back his divine new mistress in the capacity of begum number four. There was an outcry in the state palace over the defiling presence of this "foreign" woman, and hence the nawab was forced to settle his Oriental bloom in the more liberal environs of Delhi. Her palace is now our hotel; its name recalls her favorite flower.

The current owner bought the building from the nawab (it took the usual route: gambling, alcohol, women, and finally a distress sale) and had it lovingly restored, from the seventy-five-year-old marble fountain at the entrance to the high ceiling fans in the rooms, coupled with the latest modern facilities like central air-conditioning and Jacuzzi-enabled bathtubs. Since it is a heritage site, the facade was left untouched, but the interiors are a blend of antique and modern. The original flooring in Italian marble has been retained, as has the semiprecious inlay work on the pillars. Huge bay windows dominate the spacious lobby and flood it with natural light, while the beautifully landscaped exterior provides the perfect backdrop for this little nugget in the midst of a very polluted New Delhi.

———

When I walk in that morning, Rishi waves to me; he is anxious for me to join him at Reception. "The guest in room 235 is *so* single, darling," Rishi says, leaning over the counter. Rishi is the repository of all guest information. He is the executive housekeeper at the Grand Orchid, so he has far-reaching powers—i.e., powers that extend right into the guest's bedroom. And if there is one place Rishi or his alter ego "Princess Chiniqua" is comfortable in, it is a man's bedroom.

"How do you know?" I ask despite myself.

"Well, no wedding band for one."

"So?"

"Oh, please, Aisha. Just how many single male guests check in their wedding bands along with their baggage?" Rishi cocks an eyebrow at me.

This is true. More often than not, the norm is for married men to relegate the band to the second drawer of the bedside table—the one right under the dials for the music system.

"Okay, so tell me." I surrender.

"Did a whole sweep, darling. No wedding band anywhere, not even in the drawer. No photographs on the bedside table, laundry clear of all female remnants—perfume, lipstick stains . . ."

"Stop! This is too much," I say dramatically, clapping my hands over my ears.

"Oh, you *so* want to hear this." He pauses for impact. "No long late-night phone calls either."

Phone calls are my area; the hotel operators

report them to me. "Hey, that's beyond your juris-
diction," I say territorially.

"Oh, please, get over it! I spoke with Neerja."
Neerja is the chief telephone operator. "She confirmed all. Seems our man has a sexy voice too."

This is great. Now the depleted reserves of eligible men have to be shared with the fellas as well.

"Why don't we just send out a group page and
inform everyone, 'Hot man in house,'" I snap and
am about to turn back to the file I've just opened
when Misha calls to tell me that Anushka's divorce is
nearly final; the happily married one among us is
squarely on the raft again.

Let's be honest here: Divorce, which clouds most
people in despair, brings some good "indications"
for us single gals. The newly divorced guys—I call
them the "second sherwani" guys, ready for their
second *sherwani*, the groom's outfit—may take their
time doing it the second time around, but when they
do, it's likely to be the real deal. Besides, people with
a track record of marital failure are far more motivated to succeed than those who've never been married.

Anushka dated Anuj for six years through high
school and college before marrying him. She was our
poster child for "love conquers all" until about eight
months ago, when she decided to surprise him on
their anniversary while he was on a business trip
to Mumbai. At the hotel, the nice young lady at

Reception inquired if she was there to see Mr. or *Mrs.* Mishra.

I received her distress call and told her to wait in the hotel bar while I made calls to verify if there was a Mrs. Mishra staying at the hotel. To cut a long story short, Anushka soon turned into the poster child for the newly-single-again community.

Anushka works at a garment export house and is thirty years old, very attractive, with straight hair that looks just as gorgeous worn loose as when wrapped in a chignon. She is blessed with a sharp nose and a high forehead, not to mention perfect cheekbones. She is one of those women who gets more beautiful with the passage of time.

That evening we meet for our weekly coffee indulgence at the neighborhood Barista, and for once Anushka, usually reticent, holds forth. "I'll kill the bastard!" she announces, shaking with anger in her sexy, fitted jeans and six-inch stilettos, which are sharp enough to serve as instruments of torture.

"What's he done now?" I ask as Misha and I exchange a worried glance.

"He sent some goons to pick up the car! It's registered in his name. They were proper goondas. I can't believe he is being so petty!"

"Well, you are trying to divorce him, it's not going to be pretty," I say, stating the obvious.

"But I need the damn car!"

"Just buy another one. That gold color is so Lajpat Nagar Punju...." In her quest for the perfect groom, Misha has divided her community into districts, neighborhoods, color schemes, car preferences, financial net worth, and so on. To her credit, it's a really exhaustive feasibility study. And she's usually dead on when it comes to spotting potential desi-dulha (Indian groom) material.

"Anyway," I butt in before Misha launches into one of her speeches, "you don't need him or his car. He's not your meal ticket and never was."

"Cut the feminist crap! What I need right now is good old-fashioned revenge."

"Since when—"

"Talk to me, sister," interjects Misha, pushing me roughly aside. Her eyes are alight. I really don't like where this is heading, but I am obviously in the minority.

"Well, I have it all planned, and if you guys are game, tonight's the night," Anushka purrs.

"Count me in. I can't wait to get him for what he's done. I'm surprised it took you so long." Misha, never one to mince words, is just the potion Anushka needs.

Two pairs of eyes turn toward me. We have been best friends since third grade. What the hell. I decide to comply.

"So it's all set. I'll pick you guys up at a quarter to ten tonight and then we'll head for the club. It's a Thursday, so Anuj will be there playing his usual game of squash."

"What are we going to do?" I ask anxiously.

"Just wait and watch, love," Anushka replies with a smug smile.

———

The venue is the Metropolitan Club, a haven for
the swish set. We used to go there for Sunday brunch
when Anushka was still Mrs. Mishra. It's good fun
to sit out in the sun on a wintry afternoon and take in
the sights. The club has managed to retain its colo-
nial feel with "bearers," not stewards, serving you;
the landscaped lawn is incongruously embellished
with crested paper napkins. The patrons are a mix of
new and old money, the distinction starkly evident
when the nouveaux use the generic "bearer" as opposed to the more personalized "Bahadur" or
"Rama" when summoning the stewards.

Anuj is a relatively new member of this distin-
guished club. He was twenty-one when his father
qualified as a member, and he soon discovered that
in these anointed circles, money wasn't enough to
warrant acceptance. Anushka, however, more than
made up for his lack of social pedigree and occasional awkwardness by endearing herself to the staff.
When she was around, they were guaranteed decent
service.

The kindness that Anushka reserved for the staff
was rarely on display where her poor husband was
concerned. She teased him mercilessly about the way
he matched his shirt to his shorts and his socks to
his shoes for his weekly squash-playing jaunts. I
didn't blame her, really, she was just tired of his
desperate need to fit in. He was the kind of person
who obsessed about his place in the social pecking
order. I personally felt that Anuj was better off not
being a member. But then where else can you get
chicken tikka that costs the same as in a Pandara

Park restaurant, served in the ambience of a gentle-men's club? Not to mention the sheer snob value. Post the breakup, naturally, we are no longer entitled to the succulent benefits of the chicken tikka, and haven't been to the club in months.

But here we are now, headed back to the Metro-politan. I am not sure what to expect, but just in case we need to execute a quick getaway into the night, I dress in dark colors. Besides, it's slimming.

As I zip up my black boots, I hear the impatient honking of Anushka's car. She is punctual for the first time in many years. Misha is already seated next to her. So there are to be no stops on the way to the club. There is no escape route.

"So what's the plan?"

"We are rolling his car, toilet-paper rolling." Misha giggles.

My hand instinctively reaches for the door han-dle. "Come on, guys! Just how juvenile is that!" But the car is already swinging onto the main road. "Can't we just flatten the tires or something?"

"That wouldn't make such a spectacle of him," Anushka reasons without emotion.

I look at the large cardboard box next to me. There are two dozen rolls of toilet paper in it. I curse myself for getting into this at all. I am never comfort-able at these fancy clubs, and the thought of being caught with a roll of toilet paper in my hand is morti-fying.

"How do we intend to carry this out?"

"Well, the parking area is not very well lit and Anuj parks his car at one end, adjacent to the squash courts, where it's always deserted. I called home to make sure he'd left at the usual time, which means he will be done by ten-thirty. So we have at least twenty minutes, though we need only ten." Anushka has planned this with the precision of a professional sting operation. I am impressed despite my misgivings.

We enter the club, and as Anushka predicted, his car is parked at a deserted spot next to one other car. A very fancy other car, some sort of sports model.

"That's a 911 Turbo!" Misha blurts out, reading our minds. It is amazing how much she knows about these things, from lipsticks to sports cars. She is like the oracle on lifestyle indulgences.

We pull in on the right side of Anuj's car, and my heart starts to beat a little faster. We haven't "rolled" anyone in years. We get to work quickly, like those wheely guys at a race car rally. Soon I begin to enjoy myself. I position myself on one side of the car, and Anushka and Misha throw the rolls across to me. In seven minutes, we are nearly done. The car looks like a mechanical mummy, and we still have two rolls left. Misha throws me one roll, and in trying to catch it, I bump against the fancy car behind me. Suddenly, a shrill sound rents the silent night; it is the friggin' car alarm.

"Aisha, hurry, get over here!" Anushka and Misha yell as they pile into the car.

But I can't move. Here's the problem: In high-stress situations, I freeze. So I just stand there rooted to the ground, eyes trained on the fancy car like I can stop the alarm telepathically or something. Suddenly, this gorgeous hunk emerges from the shadows. He is truly beautiful: smooth olive skin, high cheekbones with eyebrows doing an arch worthy of SRK, Shah Rukh Khan, India's hottest movie star. He looks at me with a quizzical expression. I mutter something inadequate, fling the toilet paper at him, and suddenly galvanized, turn on my heels. He catches the roll with one hand and calls out as I stumble into the car, and the three of us roar away.

Anushka and Misha are in the throes of giggly delirium; I am in shock. I can't believe that the best-looking man I've ever laid eyes on has been witness to me doing a version of the Grateful Dead with a roll of toilet paper in my hands.

"Ladies, that was a success. *Uski band baja di.*" Anushka giggles. "It was worth every minute. I just wish I could see Anuj's face when he sees the car."

Misha then turns around to look at me. "Hello, Aisha, Aisha, Earth calling Aisha, are you there?"

"Yep, I'm here. That was something, wasn't it? Did you see that guy who showed up? I hope he doesn't complain."

"Well, if he does, it will be only about you, 'cuz he got a good look at you. We were already safe in the car," Misha says.

I realize I'll never be able to go back to that club again.

Anuj discovers the car shortly after we drive off, because fifteen minutes later he calls Anushka and accuses her of damaging his car, which she of course denies. Finally, in exasperation, he gets into his car after impatiently unwrapping the driver's side. He doesn't know it then, but it is going to be a long night for him. As he speeds home with the dexterity of a race car driver, the thullas spot him and pull him over. When the cops say that they are "with you for you always," they seem to mean it. Certainly, they are with Anuj for a long time that night.

The Naked Truth

I love the Grand Orchid in the mornings: the dewy, freshly scrubbed look, the lingering smell of carpet shampoo, and the slickness of the freshly polished marble floor. Mornings at the hotel are really the best time; you can enjoy the beauty and sheer opulence of the place without any intrusion from the guests. Often, very early in the morning, toward the end of my night shift, I kick off my shoes and glide around barefoot, the cool Italian marble sending a tingle through my soles. I like to imagine that this is how princesses of yore cooled their feet, dancing to the ethereal melody of a ghazal exquisitely rendered by a court poet, the sound of their anklets resonating through the palace. I normally have only Kenny G for company, and, of course, the boss's diktats to make me run around, but at least the flooring is top grade.

When I enter the Grand Orchid that morning, I am still breathless from the experience of the previous night. It's not like we've never done crazy, juvenile, irresponsible things before, it's just that I've never been caught in the act—and by the most gorgeous man ever! I go to the locker room to change into my sari and look at the disappointing silhouette I make in the mirror. Is it really necessary to look exactly the way one feels, sort of dumpy and sleepy? Despairingly, I slip on my walking shoes instead of the regulation heels. The red Reebok pair are flat, comfortable, well worn, and cleverly disguised by the uneven fall of my sari. And they are perfect for the first task of the day that my boss has lovingly picked out for me.

You see, according to my boss D. P. Gupta's carefully laid-out plan, I am to start the morning shift with a stroll down the guest corridors, to check that all breakfast order cards have been picked off the doorknobs. Then I am to compile a list of the erring stewards who missed a doorknob and ensure that the boss's hit list for the day is complete, thus giving him something to do and someone to rant against. I pull out my list of rooms and set about ticking off names against a list, exhaling audibly when I discover that the breakfast cards have not been collected from the fourth floor. I hate getting people into trouble.

I descend to the third floor and commence my inspection. I am at the corner where the deluxe rooms give on to the private terrace gardens when an unexpected gust of wind blows the paper from my hand. I watch its flight over the little balustrade that cordons off the corridor from the beautifully manicured lawn. It sways and settles onto the grass. I let out a cry of exasperation and decide that the only option is to make the undignified climb over the partition to retrieve the paper. I take a quick look around and hoist up my sari. I know I look quite a sight in my sneakers, but the time is for action and not vanity. Besides, it is 6 A.M. and there is not a fly in sight.

I climb over the balustrade with ease and make my way across the grass, aware that the sprinkler timers are set for six-fifteen. I hold my sari up to my knees and sprint toward the offending piece of paper. I am about to scoop it up with my free hand when I see a flash of white. I look up instinctively and encounter a sight that is not meant for the fainthearted. A well-proportioned man is standing in the sun in all his morning glory. The flash of white was the towel he discarded while staring out into the garden, stark naked. I stare right back at him, gawk actually, and am about to express outrage at his audacity when I realize that I am the offender. This is his space and I am the intruder. So I do what any self-respecting woman in my situation would do. I bolt, Reebok, sari, paper, and all.

I climb back over the balustrade and run all the way down to the fire exit, not wanting to risk waiting for the elevator. This could mean major trouble, possibly the pink slip. "Oh, God," I pray. "Please help me, please get me out of this, for I have sinned. Not only have I dared to flout grooming standards and worn sneakers with my sari, I have strayed into a guest's private space and peeked at his privates!"

I reach the lobby level in record time, breathless with anxiety. I fish out my mobile phone and go to my usual hangout, the luggage room. Crouching behind a guest's oversize and clearly well-used Vuitton, I speed-dial Misha. She answers after eighteen rings.

"It had to be you."

"Yeah, who else do you know who's poor enough to need to work at six in the morning?" I crib. Then I tell her why I have every bloody reason to feel sorry for myself. I am most certainly going to be sacked in the next couple of hours. The only question is, Should I wait it out and have Security assist me in clearing out my locker, or should I help myself and get it over with?

"Hmm, so he was like *totally* naked?" Misha is wide awake now.

"Yes," I repeat.

"Wow, so is he like, you know, hung and stuff?"

"Hung? I'm sorry, I wasn't really focusing on the details. I was too shocked, and I really don't give a damn if he's hung like a horse! I need to figure out a way to save my job. What if he complains?"

"Then counteraccuse," Misha the amoralist replies smoothly. "Maybe he's a nudist or something and he does this to make people feel uncomfortable."

"No, see, there is a problem with that logic. He was where he was meant to be; I was the one staring in, you know, invading his privacy! Have you heard of Peeping Toms?"

"Oh, Peeping Toms are men. Aisha, stop being paranoid."

I absorb Misha's amazing logic and decide to let her resume her beauty sleep. I'll just have to brave the consequences. This too will pass. It has to, right? And I finally have the answer to one of life's greater questions: There *is* something more embarrassing than being found mummifying a car.

For the next hour, I labor over finding the right explanation for spying on a guest and then decide to sharpen my excuse-making faculties with a cup of tea. It is a quarter to nine and the cafeteria is a flurry of activity with people sipping their last cuppa before starting work.

On the way to the tea machine, I have to walk past the most powerful mafia in the hotel biz, the secretaries. The grandes dames are seated in order of importance: Rosie, the owner's secretary, twenty-six years at the hotel; Jayanti, the GM's secretary, eighteen years in the hotel biz; Madhu, secretary of the director of sales, with twelve years' experience; and finally Sarla, who has been working for the director of Human Resources for fourteen years. I bow my head deferentially and flash them my most obsequious smile. Rosie narrows her eyes and waves me over. Shit! Today is just not my day.

As I make my way to the circle of the Holy Cows, I promise myself that I'll think before I speak. The secs come with a HWC (Handle with Care) sticker, and it is rumored that careers are sealed with a nod of the head or a discreet word to the boss.

"Good morning," I say to no one in particular, while making eye contact with Rosie. (I have learned some of the tricks of the trade. She gloats at my subtle favoritism.)

"How are you, young lady?" she asks over the rim of her coffee mug.

"Very well, ma'am. Busy, of course."

"That's because your boss doesn't do any work," she remarks with a little laugh and a flick of her hand.

My career is already precariously placed; I have no intention of getting embroiled in any word games. But I am also not above letting the world in on my boss's frailties. "He has many priorities," I say with a giggle, much to the amusement of my eager audience.

My boss is a known philanderer, although he has never tried his tricks with me. I don't know whether to be offended or relieved by this. He is not known to be discriminating and yet he passed me up.

"Naughty girl, run along now." Sarla dismisses me as the others begin to gather their assortment of bags, umbrellas, and mobile phones.

I leave with a smile fixed on my face. That went pretty well. Maybe I can hit them for a favor if the boss decides to sack me.

I enter the lobby through the servants'—all right, the staff—entrance and am met with the very sight I have been dreading all morning. In the middle of the lobby, next to the ostentatious arrangement of ficus and birds-of-paradise, stand the boss and the guest I spied on earlier, in animated conversation. The two of them together look like the two ends of the evolution spectrum. One is a fine specimen of manhood—okay, I confess, I got a *really* good look—and the other is a reminder of how close we came to remaining apes. The Boss's Wicked Witch of the East lips are opening now and the words that escape his mouth have me freezing in my little red . . . shoes! Shit! I forgot to take them off!

"Aisha!" I quickly fix my sari and walk over. The guest is looking at me from under heavily lidded eyes, an arrogant tilt to his head. He is dressed in a perfectly tailored suit, probably from one of those "So & So and Brothers" on Bond Street. I know these types and totally dislike them.

The boss looks sour as always.

I am ready to throw in the towel and just admit to everything. There is really no point in trying to come up with pathetic excuses. "I'm sor—"

"Aisha, meet Mr. Verma. He is staying with us for three months. He's just moved to India."

"Good morning," I say, daring to look at him, and then I almost freeze. I can feel my face turning pale. Omigod. This is the dude from the night before.

"Morning," he replies curtly, his eyes fixed on my little red sneakers.

I step back two paces, hoping that this will help conceal my irreverent footwear and diminish the chances of him recognizing me. "Mr. Verma wishes to change his room. I told him we would be glad to, only this room has one of the best views."

"Absolutely," I reply, quickly picking up a travel brochure from the desk and trying to conceal my face behind it.

"From the inside looking out or the outside looking in?" Mr. Verma's words are glacial.

"Ah . . . uh . . . I . . ." I can't think of a way to extricate myself from this impossible predicament.

"Right." He shuts me up abruptly. "I want it changed. Privacy is definitely an issue. I suppose Ms. Aisha can arrange it today. She knows which room I'm in. I'll pick up the keys in the evening." And with a brief nod of the head, Mr. Verma stalks off. I should be grateful to him for sparing my job, but his arrogance only makes me fume.

"Nice man, real classy," the boss says, taking in his retreating figure.

I roll my eyes in response. I can't trust myself to speak.

"Aisha," says my nice, understanding boss, "don't get into your bitchy spinster mode. He's paying three hundred fifty dollars a night. I want no complaints, understood?"

The rest of the day is spent avoiding Mr. Verma. I am grateful he hasn't placed me as the crazy female trying to toilet-roll a car, and I don't want to do anything to jog his memory.

I find a use today for things I never appreciated before: pillars, great to back up against; flower arrangements with huge ficus leaves and spiky things, which I duck behind thrice when danger threatens, nearly impaling myself in the process. And, of course, the luggage room, which is my haven. I am creeping out of it, ready to make a mad dash for the pillar with the flower arrangement, and wishing for potted plants on wheels I can push along to the exit now that my shift is finally over, when Karan Verma comes up from behind and taps me on my shoulder.

"Excuse me, miss."

I screech to a halt on the marble floor and turn around. "Mrs." I smile. I don't know why I say it. I don't even know what point I am trying to make. Maybe I am trying to say that I am not quite a sex-deprived voyeur.

"Uh-huh," he replies disinterestedly. "I need a favor."

No. "Certainly." I smile.

He thrusts a list at me. Oh God, he writes out lists on his personal letterhead! I have to stop myself from sniffing it for musk or some other male scent. "This," he explains with the patience of one talking to a two-year-old, "is a list of people I will need to send gifts to over the next three months." He pauses. I nod to indicate comprehension. "Flowers, perfume where mentioned. You do international, right?" He looks at me doubtfully.

"Yes, sir." In fact, we do one better than

"international," we specialize in housing international jerks of the sort he is turning out to be.

"Great, I want you to take care of it." Then he looks me squarely in the eye. "Just don't gift-wrap it in toilet paper," he says sardonically as he turns on his heels and walks off.

The Wild, Wild Web

Misha and I are at one of those Wi-Fi coffee bars and We Have Mail.

"Look, this guy has expressed an interest in you!" Misha says, sipping on her latte. "That means he's looked at your profile, likes the initial brief, and wants you to check out his details. So all we have to do is click on the link—"

As Misha launches into the etiquette of online spouse hunting, I reflect that although I am a reluctant party—well, almost—this is my new reality.

"Oh, no, he's not right at all," Misha groans, referring to the first victim.

"Who?"

"This guy, Rakesh. He's thirty-three, lives in Bhilai . . . Where's that? Anyway, he's a divorcé with two children. He's looking for a 'bold' girl and thinks you might be a match."

I burst out laughing. "Not quite Birmingham, is it? Any guy who specifies 'bold' in his requirements is not really looking to make an honest woman out of you."

"Really, Aisha, had you put in your photograph, someone more eligible would have expressed an interest."

"Oh, this really works, Mish. Just how many men are beating down *your* door?"

"Well, since you ask, there's one very interesting option."

"I am all ears. Pray tell."

"His name is Deep. He's a cut surd—one of those Sikhs who have cut their long hair short and don't wear turbans. You know how cute those are! I haven't seen his pix, but then these guys are genetically favored. He lives and works in Florida with Microsoft. We have actually spoken once and he has the cutest twang."

I have to grudgingly admit that this doesn't sound quite as hopeless as my option. "So what's next?"

"He's coming to Mumbai next week, we'll meet then. He's sending me a ticket," she says, swiveling in her chair to face the computer.

"Whoa, hold on . . . Doesn't this sound too well timed?" I spin her around to face me. "He's sending you a ticket to visit him and that's okay with you? I'm sure he'll expect something in return. Have you stopped to think about that?"

"Come on! He wants to send me a ticket because

he's here for work and can't travel around. I go in the morning, return at night, finito."

"What if he's a psycho or something?" I say, refusing to let go.

"Then I'll ditch him at the airport. You know I have the right instincts. I'll just spend the rest of the day shopping. Mumbai is great for accessories. Do you think he'll send me a ticket on one of those no-frills airlines?" Misha asks with a look of utter distaste. I am still contemplating an appropriate answer to that question when she continues. "Because if he does, I'm not going."

"All right then, let the record state that I have a problem with this," I say, really annoyed, yet not willing to lock horns with my closest friend.

Things usually have a way of sorting themselves out. In a reversal of plans, Deep decides to come to Delhi after all, so Misha doesn't have to travel to Mumbai. And he finally sends a photograph of himself. It is a passport shot, and honestly, he misses the cuteness measure by a mile. It appears as if he swam away from the gene pool that Misha so counted on. She is extremely disappointed, but I decide not to be a damp squib for once and assure her that passport shots are almost always unflattering. My passport has a shot of me in my teens, when I was going through a really bad perm phase—a very Medusa-like style that I got at the price of six months' savings and a severe tongue-lashing from my folks. I had also discovered kajal around the same time, and the entire effect was very Cleopatra Gets Zapped. But I take it in stride, and every time an immigration officer asks if that is really me, I tell him it is quite the story of the ugly duckling.

Deep is to get in on Saturday and our entire life becomes a countdown to D-day. Misha, the eternal optimist, conveniently convinces herself that there is an Adonis hidden behind that shot. Besides, you can't judge a movie by its trailer. And, of course, the fun always lies more in the anticipation, etc., etc. . . . She is already planning her wardrobe for the day.

The salon appointment is fixed, the nail bar visited, and the only detail pending is the outfit. It is going to be brand new and completely off-the-rack. Misha has just lost four kilos, courtesy of the GM diet—a different food group each day—and has to acquire a tighter pair of jeans.

"Second skin, baby, second skin," Misha announces triumphantly as we enter the hallowed archways of her church, known to the rest of us as the Oasis Mall.

My philosophy in clothes is simple: They should be the frame to my personality, thank you, Oprah. My frame is, as I like to say, a little large in the Indian context. But in some Eastern European countries or, say in the Amazon, I could be classified as petite.

While Misha tries on jeans, I turn around and make my way to the more egalitarian shoe section. I love shoes. No matter what weight, height, age, or stage of life you are in, your shoe size never changes. Shoes truly emancipate women. They don't care what you had for dinner last night, or even for the last five years, they still fit. How many times have you heard someone say, "Ooh, she is too old to wear those shoes!"

"So, how do these look?" Misha asks when I return after dropping one-sixth of my salary on a pair of two-toned stilettos.

When you go shopping with Misha and she tries something on, the thing to remember is, the problem is always with the outfit, not with her. I don't advocate dishonesty among friends, but tact is a highly underrated virtue.

"They're too eighties." Translation: They're way too tight, even minus the four kilos. "You need one of those low-waisted numbers."

"You think?" Misha does a little pirouette in front of the mirror. "You're right, I don't know why they stock this stuff."

Simple. Because the rest of the world fits into it!

We run through a dozen pairs of jeans before she settles on the perfect fit. As Misha maxes out—"Oh, shit"—her credit card, I silently hope this guy is worth it. Having okayed the photograph despite my earlier reservations, I feel somewhat culpable. But, at least, I can't be accused of being a damp squib.

Every time D. P. Gupta sees me on the phone, he assumes that I am taking a personal call. Truth be told, I have very good phone etiquette. You know, the whole smile-in-the-voice bit? I actually *practice* it. The flip side of this is that the most routine work calls may easily be mistaken from a distance for an animated conversation with a friend. Then again, for some reason, my phone always seems to ring when my boss is in the vicinity, and I have to try very hard to pretend the call is an official one when it isn't. He is right there that morning checking my emails when my cell phone rings and my I'm-married-and-hence-my-life-is-perfect older cousin Lata Didi calls.

"What are you doing?" The inquisition begins even before the "Hello."

"Ensuring that the party of twelve from China isn't served instant noodles for breakfast. Whose breakfast have you been fixing this beautiful morning? Must be the husband's."

"Very funny. I was wondering if you wanted to come over for dinner tonight?"

"Thanks, but I have plans." Lata Didi can be sweet sometimes; it is just that she behaves like she has all the answers.

"Look, I know Sachin and I have been busy this last week, but you know we are there for you and if you need anything, just let us know." Lata Didi and I don't particularly like each other and yet I have to endure the awkwardness each time she tries to be nice to me.

"Hey, it's okay. I've had a couple of boozy nights and am off food." I know the word *boozy* will kill all signs of pity. My cousin is a teetotaler. She feels that giving in to alcohol is a sign of weakness: a result of the fast life in the big city.

"Oh, well, Aisha. I don't know why I worry about

you. Just don't worry, maasi, okay, and do think about settling down now."

The resignation in my cousin's voice is completely unanticipated. I expect her to launch into her usual sermon with the fervor of a Baptist preacher. Seizing the opportunity for an exit, I say quickly, "Lata Didi, I have a call waiting. I'm expecting an international call. I have to run. Ciao."

"Bye, Aisha." She sighs.

I know I shouldn't lie—she is trying to be decent, after all—but I just can't continue with a conversation that challenges my ability to say the same things in different ways. I already spend enough time doing that all day at work.

I hang up gratefully and the phone rings again the same instant. D.P. shoots me a seriously filthy look as I answer. "Hey, who were you talking to? Don't you know I'm at the airport? Did you speak to Shastriji? Is this the right guy for me?" Misha is getting a bit agitated as she waits for Deep at Arrivals.

"Misha, I can't ask him about my friends. He needs your date of birth, et cetera, and then he has to refer to your chart. He's not a clairvoyant. Anyway, you're about two minutes from finding out if he's the one."

"The flight's landed and I can see the passengers now. Oh my God, Aisha!" Misha exclaims.

"What happened? Is it SRK?" I ask excitedly, almost forgetting that D.P. is listening in. It is a Mumbai flight, after all. Besides, the "Oh my God!" is only reserved for SRK. Chocolate mud pies and SRK.

"No, stupid! It's him and he's just like the photograph, only worse!" Misha says in disgust.

"Come on . . . take a good look. Don't be hasty and don't refer to him as 'it,' " I say.

"Okay, okay, then, he's *horrendous*! Oh God, what do I do? I'm leaving. He hasn't seen me yet!"

"Stop right there, Mish! You can't do this, he doesn't know anyone here. It's not fair. So he's not attractive, but he might be interesting. Don't stand him up." I actually feel sorry for poor Deep.

"Shoot, he's seen me! No way out now, he's waving. . . . *Yikes* . . . He has six fingers! Call me in fifteen minutes."

No way. D.P.G. is hovering in earnest. And then, all of a sudden, he decides to chat me up. "So, Ms. Bhatia, how are we today?" says the boss in a tone like that of artificial sweetener. You know, the kind that leaves a bitter aftertaste.

"Very well, sir, thank you." I try putting on my best act.

"Would you like to go get a smoke?"

Wow! This is something else! He never goes on a smoke break with me. The Smokers' Club, an exclusive meeting point for the who's who in the office, is off-limits for lesser mortals. He never includes me in it, although I am a potential pack-carrying member.

The Smokers' Club is like a parallel organization with its own system of hierarchy. It is also the place to network. How else would someone in the kitchen know a person in Accounts, or a line manager connect with a senior manager? There must have been a cigarette borrowed, or a light offered, which initiated the bond. And when it comes to promotions, guess who's first in line? Definitely the one who for months faithfully lent the crabby, and sometimes stingy, divisional head a smoke.

As the corporate world denounces its smokers, they band together and form this invisible—okay, the cloud of smoke gives them away sometimes!— yet formidable coterie. And here is the boss asking me to join him in a smoke, the corporate equivalent of the peace pipe. The fact that his regular hangers-on are not around is only a minor detail. Who knows, this could just be the beginning of a beautiful friend- ship, a turning point in our troubled relationship.

"I hope you have cigarettes on you. I've run out."

So that's it! He wants to bum a cigarette off me. Fabulous. The rest of the conversation between Marlboro Man and me is as sticky as ever. The time I come in, the time I leave, the time I go for a break, the time I spend on the phone. You know what they say, since mothers can't be everywhere, God created bosses.

"Thanks, Aisha," D. P. Gupta says, taking one last long drag. "Keep off the phone and work the floor. I'm heading home." The hell he is. He's headed straight for his mistress's arms. The oily, philandering little cheat.

"Good night, sir." I fake a smile as I drop my cig- arette and grind it under my heel.

"Now, now, Aisha, in the ashtray," D.P. says, as he waddles across the aisle with disapproval plas- tered across his face. As I bend to pick up the ciga- rette butt, I find his, dropped carelessly outside the ashtray. I nearly call out to him but check myself just in time.

Unfortunately, with age comes restraint.

I don't use the telephone till the doorman ascertains that the boss's chariot has left the premises. And then I grab it. "Mish, where are you?"

"I'm at the Big Chill. Thanks for remembering to call me."

"I'm sorry, my boss was spending some quality time with me. So, where is your friend?"

"Gone to the restroom. Aman—you remember my cousin?—I asked him to join us. I can't be alone with this guy . . . he's too strange . . . constantly doing this twitchy thingy."

"Twitchy thingy?"

"Like he's got something in his eye and needs to get it out."

"Oh, that kind of twitchy thingy." I would, under normal circumstances, have said "I told you so," but since I sanctioned his visit, that right has been lost. "He's obviously no SRK, but you liked his voice, remember? The cute twang?" I say, playing the optimist.

"Oh, that! I think he picked it up at one of those schools in Ludhiana. You know, the ones that prep you up for immigration interviews," she says, sounding quite sure of herself. One thing I have to give her credit for: Character profiling is her forte. "I should have abandoned the idea after seeing the photograph. Why did I listen to you?"

"Misha, it's not always about looks or strange twitches or accents." I sound insincere, even to myself.

"Fine, then, how about this? I call for the bill, right, and he doesn't offer to pay, or even split it. Can you imagine that? Does not lift a finger!"

"Not even the sixth one?" It's a weak attempt at humor.

She doesn't laugh. "No. I wasn't carrying much cash and you know I've maxed out my credit card. Thank God for Aman."

In the dating world you can forgive a lot of things, but a cheapskate is definitely persona non grata.

The Tao of Anushka

*I*t's a Saturday, and Anushka has already called five times. She has asked us to come with her to the opening of a new lounge bar called Tao. She often gets invited to these cool places and we always tag along. But this time she is in a dilemma after finding out that Anuj, her erstwhile spouse, is also going to grace the occasion.

"You've been doing so well, what happened now?" I ask with concern.

"I don't know. I can't bear to be around him at a social do. There will be so many common acquaintances. It's embarrassing, and he'll probably be there with some tart!"

"So what if he is? You have to get used to seeing him around, unless you plan on moving. Come on, it'll be fun, let's just go." I know it's hard for my friend. I wish I could do something to make it easier, but she needs to ride this one out on her own.

We agree to meet at eight-thirty. After much debate, I settle on a dragon-red dress with a Chinese collar that stops just short of the knees. The fabric has a subtle paisley print in the same color, and I pair it with red satin stilettos, and dress my hair in a chignon that is held in place with chopsticks. Even if I say so myself, the effect is quite eye-catching.

Anushka looks stunning in a gold off-the-shoulder top, coupled with a formfitting pair of black trousers. Misha is in her second-skin jeans, which now look as if they were grafted on. Needless to say, very soon they will be relegated to the darkest corner of Misha's abundant closet.

"Don't we look like Charlie's Angels, especially with you doing the Lucy Liu bit," Misha says, nudging me.

"I just thought it would be in sync with the general flava of the evening! The club's name is Tao, right?" I ask, suddenly unsure and feeling a bit wannabe.

"I'm only teasing, Aisha. It's really cute. Besides, where else can you go wearing a Chinese collar nowadays?"

"Meow . . . Ladies, can we save the cat fight till after the party? It's always more fun after a couple of drinks," Anushka chimes in. I straighten my shoulders. I must be looking good, or Misha would never have made that crack. So it's a little unconventional, but then so am I.

The problem with three single women entering a party unescorted is that everyone, men and women alike, look at you with these cash-register eyes swiftly totaling up your assets. It's like "let's give the face an eight," "the ass a seven," "the grand total being . . ." It's unnerving if you're new to the game, but when you've been single for as long as we have, you get used to it. Besides, once you are comfortably ensconced in a corner, it's fun to do it to others.

The obvious victims are the new entrants making their debut in the social jungle. They get spotted as soon as they walk into a room, which makes them extremely self-conscious, of course, and very aware of their short skirts and transparent straps. In a desperate attempt to blend in, they desperately try to flick away imaginary locks of hair: the glorious feminine equivalent of the nervous male tic.

We, on the other hand, walk in with aplomb. I look around hoping to see someone I know and am almost turning away when I see Nic and Ric heading straight for us. Don't get me wrong, I love these guys to death, but the problem is that we always end up superglued at these sorts of dos. And their touchy-feely presence has the ability to get rid of any straight men within sneezing distance.

"Darling, aren't you the little geisha tonight!" exclaims Ric.

"You think? I left the white face and Tweety Bird lips at home, decided to go casual tonight."

"So, is Anuj here?" Anushka jumps in. It has been playing on her mind all day long, and she needs to get it over with.

"He's at the bar, on the other side. Don't think he's seen you yet. You look stunning," says Nic, taking both her hands in his.

"Thanks, Nic. Well, that decides it. Here's where I'm operating from tonight," Anushka says, settling into a beanbag.

Leaving her in the safe custody of Nic, the rest of us find our way to the bar. I decide to go fruity and order a peach daiquiri. Named after an obscure Cuban river, the daiquiri's peachy version is the yummiest.

"I rather like the banana flavor," Ric purrs pointedly at the cute bartender.

Just then a familiar voice calls out over my shoulder, "Aisha? Fancy seeing you here." I recognize the voice all too well, but in the subdued lighting, I have to squint a little to take in the face. It is Anuj, and as my eyes adjust to his globular nose and bushy eyebrows, I catch the outline of another familiar male silhouette. *Shoot! I have to stop thinking of him naked! He has a face, not just a body.*

"Hi," I respond to Anuj. I am embarrassed by my thoughts and refuse to look at anything other than the man's shoes.

"This is my friend Karan Verma. He's just moved here from New York."

"Hi, umm . . ." My gaze slowly follows the crease of his trousers and stalls at an inappropriate place as I search for something socially apt to say.

"We've met before . . ." Karan Verma says.

I nod in response. "He's staying at the Orchid," I tell Anuj.

"And I'm familiar with her artwork." Karan Verma looks me straight in the eye. "Tell me, do you work in two- or three-ply?"

"You are doing *art* these days, Aisha?" Anuj asks curiously.

"Only when I am truly inspired," I answer pointedly.

Karan Verma smiles at me lazily, and just as I am readying myself to give it back to him, I feel a jab in the small of my back. Ric and Misha. Rule number one of friendship among singles: Never hog a good-looking man. You never know who may have their sights set on him. It's sort of like equal-opportunity dating. Friends are more important than a man any day—especially this sarcastic man.

Anuj spares me the bother of making the introductions by grabbing Misha and launching into the long-time-no-see routine. Except it leaves me face-to-face with Karan Verma.

"Must you insist on stripping me with your eyes?" he says without preamble.

"*Excuse* me?" I mutter.

"I have never ever been so stared at." He towers over me, his lips pursed in mild disdain. I really don't know what to say and look up at him feeling mortified and guilty. Maybe I should just apologize for everything—for seeing him naked, for staring at him, for cursing him under my breath, for global warming, for Osama still being on the sprint. *Just apologize for everything, Aisha, and get it over with!*

My thoughts are interrupted by the sound of him chuckling. "Actually, I love being objectified. And thinking of all the wicked ways in which you want to have your way with me. . . ."

"I want no such thing!"

"Yes, you do."

"No, I don't."

"I think you do."

"That's because you think you are some sort of sex god!"

"No, I don't, but you do," he counters.

"Oh, this conversation is so ridiculous!"

"I agree with you."

"You do?"

"Absolutely. But any time you want a test drive, let me know—assuming, of course, you are satisfied with what you've seen."

"The nerve . . ." I turn around in a huff.

As I walk away, I can feel his eyes boring into my back and the disdainful snigger he is trying to control. The temptation to turn and flee is strong, but this is not a classic Bollywood moment, and I am no

Bollywood bimbette. So I turn around deliberately and walk straight back up to him. I hold his eyes as I reach behind him suggestively, only to pick up my cocktail glass.

"And you thought I was returning for you." I smile sweetly.

"Or to pat my luscious tush," he answers without missing a beat.

It is an open invitation to a verbal duel, but I am not to be enticed. Frankly, I am shocked that I dared to say anything at all. But then I am not at work and I can't be accused of fraternizing with the guests. Giving my hair a toss and adding that extra swing to my hips, I saunter off, reveling in the freedom of being all woman. No demure seedha pallav sari to hold back the sex appeal tonight.

I am on my fifth daiquiri when he reemerges. Why do I not hate Karan Verma at this moment? I don't know; perhaps it's the alcohol taking effect. "Hi again. How are you holding up?"

"Very well, Mr. Verma, very well." I giggle.

He sort of frowns at that one, much to my delight, but chooses to ignore it. "The name's Karan. Would you care to dance?"

"What? Are we at a debutante ball or something? It's trance music in a lounge bar, darling. Just close your eyes and move." I snort, pushing the envelope as they say.

"All right then, would you like to close your eyes and move with me?" says Karan, not waiting for a reply as he takes me into his arms and sweeps me onto the dance floor.

Very Mills and Boon, but I swear, this is how it happened . . . or is it the booze? Either way, I don't quite remember my feet carrying me there. We move together for what seems like an eternity.

"Would you like to go sit somewhere?" he asks finally. I nod, feeling a bit fuzzy, as he leads me off to a little corner with oversize cushions. It feels like we are the only two people in the world. And then I catch sight of Anushka.

She is on the dance floor, clearly high as a kite, in one of those sandwich dances, making a complete spectacle of herself. You know, the kind that's also termed a "threesome on the dance floor." The two guys are obviously enjoying themselves. Clumsily, I get on all fours in an attempt to make my way to Anushka. "I know I'm rushing off, but I need to go, it was nice, thanks."

Karan looks at me strangely, almost like he is about to pet me or something, and then abruptly stands up, holding out his hand to help me up. "So, can I have your number?"

"My extension? Just dial 0 and ask for me."

"No, I mean your personal number."

"Anuj has it. Just get it from him. Ciao."

As I rush toward Anushka, I see Anuj get there before me. The two of them exchange some words and then walk off together.

"Oh, oh!" I find Mish standing next to me.

"Where are they off to now? We don't need more drama," I say to her with a mounting sense of dread, and the two of us run after them. But it's too late. They are gone.

"Try to call her, Mish. This is such a bad idea."

Misha dials Anushka's number and speaks for less than half a minute. "She is all right and sounds sober enough. They're just talking. She says we can carry on. You want to go back in or leave?"

"I think we should leave. Just hope he gets her home safe and sound," I say, feeling worried.

I remember the day Anushka returned from that fateful Mumbai trip when she discovered that her husband was cheating on her on the eve of their sixth anniversary. All she said was that it was over, and that we were never to discuss it again. After that, life went back to normal—almost too soon, in retrospect. I thought of her stoicism as a positive thing and was proud of her for being so strong. But maybe she needed to let it out. Tonight is the first time she has come face-to-face with Anuj since their separation. Will this be the beginning of tumultuous times?

"Thank God! I've been trying to reach you for hours," I scream when Anushka finally answers the phone at eleven the next day.

"Relax, I've been sleeping." Anushka sighs.

"So, what happened?"

"Well, umm . . . nothing really. Look, I'm running a little late for work. Can we meet this evening for a drink?"

"Sure, I'll see you then."
Is Anushka being evasive or am I imagining it?

I reach the bar early and snag a nice booth by the window. TGIF is mostly a watering hole for young working people to assemble postwork and grab a couple of beers. It's a cool environment for single women: no looks, no come-ons, no free drinks. Okay, the last bit isn't the really cool part, but sometimes a girl just wants to buy her own drinks.

Tonight is one of those nights.

I look around and survey the other revelers: the loosened ties, the mussed-up hair, the jovial ribbing. One large table is occupied by a call center gang with their American host. I guess that he is down from Texas to tell "the guys what a great job they are doing down in In-deee-yah. Hee-haw, buddy!" As expected, he dominates the conversation, while the natives listen in rapt attention, trying to pick up the nuances of his Yankee twang.

Then there are the serious guys sitting crouched over their drinks in intense conversation. This species usually moves in packs of three or four. They care little about anyone else or the ambience. They never lunge for the bill: The pre-anointed one pays for the boys per rotation. Looking at them, it's safe to assume that they will, in all likelihood, head home to cozy up in their starched PJs for another conference call, probably with the business channel NDTV Profit playing on mute.

Finally, there are the dinks. They are everywhere: the malls, tennis clubs, private dinner parties; a ready reminder of how you can actually have it all—career and spouse. If you happen to be single and by some tragic accident become enmeshed in a conversation with a dink, beware of some of the recurring topics. Usually it's the holiday abroad with the husband, or if they're the supercilious variety, the girly holiday just to get away from the men, you know? *No, I don't, you have to have a man to get away from!* Or it's about the challenge of juggling marital life and a career, which of course they manage to do very successfully. *That's why they are talking about it, silly!*

As my favorite former dink walks in, I observe the surreptitiously admiring looks she gets from the men, but to me she appears tired and drawn. "So what's your poison tonight?" I ask a little too cheerfully.

"I'd like a beer, a nice chilled one."

"So pick. Is it a pitcher night or a pint one?"

"Pitcher."

After placing our orders, I turn to Anushka. "So spill it, what happened yesterday?"

"What part do you want to know about? Before or after I slept with him?" she says, getting straight to the point.

I shake my head in disbelief. "What does this mean now?"

"Nothing. It was just breakup sex."

Breakup sex? There seems to be a word for everything these days. There is "make-up sex" that follows after a tiff, and then there is "breakup sex," to say good-bye. If you ask me, people just need a reason to have sex, it's as simple as that.

"If you had to sleep with someone, why him?"

"You don't get it, Aisha. Not everything is black and white. You've never been married," Anushka says with marked irritation.

"Nor have I experienced the joys of divorce. But a little thing called common sense tells me it's a bad idea, no matter what you call it." I am angry now. How dare she look back! And how could I have been so stupid? This could have been prevented had I not been trying to relive my teens by canoodling with Karan.

"Look, please don't get mad." Her voice breaks. "It's been really hard and I needed closure. I never got that."

"You think sex will bring you closure! Are you following one of those gurus like Osho or something?"

"Aisha, hear me out. It was just sex. If men can have it, so can women. . . . It's truly over now."

As I look at my friend, I start to get it. She means every word she says. She isn't posing anymore, playing the big, strong girl. Sometimes life is like a book. You can get so desperate to reach the end of the story that you conveniently skip a couple of chapters. However, when you do get to the end, you're left with this icky restless feeling, and you know that you need to go back to those missing chapters before you can close the book.

Anushka has finally closed her book. As if on cue, the waiter arrives with our drinks. "Here's to us." I smile as we clink glasses.

Love Don't Cost a Thing

*T*hat evening, while Anushka and I mull over the vagaries of romantic love, Misha is making her own discoveries. She is off on her first date with Samir. He is an old friend of Ric's, and they were introduced the other night at Tao. Sparks flew; digits were exchanged. The initial reports were favorable, and although not the much-desired NRI, Samir is involved in a business that takes him abroad frequently.

As far as predate rituals were concerned, it was perfect. Samir called twice, asking her where she would like to go, then to get directions to where she lived. Misha lives in a cul-de-sac where all the homes are identical. Finding her residence is a challenge even for the most astute navigator. But when she offered to meet him at some familiar landmark, he declined and insisted on coming right to her door. Major brownie points!

Samir entered the gated community on time at half past eight that evening but kept going around in circles. The male of the species, as we all know, refuses to ask for directions. Twenty minutes later, feeling her foundation melt—the electricity having let her down as well—Misha took matters into her own hands and called him up. It was decided that she would wait in front of the house. Misha was hard to miss in a tight dress of the brightest pink. She had overcompensated with the heels—a common problem with the vertically challenged—and wore five-inch stilettos. So there she stood in neon pink, hands firmly glued to her hips, looking like one of those pink swans people leave out as part of the garden decor.

Misha was understandably a little upset, but her ill humor dissipated when she saw Samir pull up in a chauffeur-driven black Mercedes.

As she sank into the leather interior of the car, Misha realized that she could spend the entire evening just cruising around. The blast of the air-conditioner instantly cooled her foundation, producing an iridescent glow. Misha was pleased. No need for any of that Body Shop powder, she thought as she caught a glimpse of herself in the rearview mirror. Given an option, she always chose to sit behind the driver to keep tabs on her makeup. It also helped to control her facial expressions, a useful tool on a date.

"You look great. A slight change in plan, though.

We can't go to Mint, there's a private party on there. So I thought we could go to the Polo Club," Samir suggested.

This was bad news. Misha had dressed for a night out dancing under neon lights, and he was taking her to a gentlemen's club.

"Look, I don't really think I'm dressed for walls in mahogany. Can we go someplace else?" she pleaded.

"You look just fine," Samir assured her, squeezing her hand. "They'll love having you there."

They sure will, Misha thought.

The Polo Club is the older gentlemen's sanctuary. Very classy, very mahogany, leather, and crystal. It even has its own wine cellar, and the humidor had been introduced into the service sequence with enviable discretion.

As Misha walked in looking like a pink flamingo, heads turned. In an environment too discreet for stares, the head turning was sufficient to signal an alien in their midst. Fortunately, Samir was known and the captain quickly escorted them to a table in the corner. But to Misha, probably experiencing self-consciousness for the first time in her life, it felt like a bit of a slight. She turned to the steward and said, "No, this won't quite do. We need a better table somewhere by the fireplace."

Now, one thing Misha is not is a wallflower. No matter how out of place she felt, she was not going to be shoved into a corner. She was going to have the best table in the house!

The captain, looking a little disappointed,

shepherded them to the desired area. "Hope this is better, ma'am."

Misha gave him a "mistress of the manor" nod and settled into the comfy contours of the leather sofa. She then turned to her host for the evening and began her mental evaluation. Samir was on the positive side of the eligibility litmus. A bit yuppie in the way he dressed—the oxford blue shirt and khakis look—but there was definite potential. He was clearly a traditionalist, but not the flashy sort. No funky rings or stones worn at the urging of mummy*ji* and the family astrologer promising to calm a moody astral planet or two. We all know that I believe in astrology, it's just that I have a problem when a man wears more jewelry and rocks than I do!

So he was a moderate traditionalist. Plenty of possibilities, Misha thought with satisfaction. He had a bit of an overbite, but with the wonders of modern cosmetic dentistry, this was a small problem. For Misha, every man is a project, a diamond in the rough for her expert eye to spot and her craftmanship to shape and cut.

As Misha contemplated the makeover, Samir cut in. "What would you like to drink?" Before she could answer, he said, "How about a bottle of white wine, or do you prefer red? I think white, an Indian white," he said, directly to the captain. He smiled benignly at Misha and mistook her silence for acquiescence. Actually, Misha was in shock. She had just been steamrolled, and the rehearsed smile that one adopts on a date was frozen in place. Samir turned to the captain. "You know, I have this coupon, actually my dad got it with his membership. It entitles me to two free bottles of wine." *Wait a minute, had he also said "free" out loud? Somebody give him a thesaurus! What happened to "complimentary" or even "gratis"?*

The captain nodded with thinly veiled derision. Misha could almost read his thoughts. The staff from then on would refer to them as the "freebie table," labeled and dismissed for the rest of the evening. *We came in a Mercedes,* Misha wanted to say. But Samir was winking suggestively at Misha. "...depending on how the evening goes, we just might order the second one."

As Misha took in his toothy grin and the complimentary nuts he kept stuffing into his cranelike mouth, she cringed. Had she been five years younger, she would have walked out. But as the sea of options dries up, one learns to compromise. And people say we get more exacting with age! So he was cheap, but one had to be smart with money to be able to afford that Mercedes. "He's not cheap, he's careful," she mumbled to herself.

The evening progressed rather decently—at least for Samir. In fact, it went so well for him that he thought she was worth the second *free* bottle after all. It was quite another matter that he was doing all the drinking while Misha stayed with her first glass. The one thing we girls know is our alcohol; if it has to be Indian wine, it has to be Sula. This wasn't Sula. So Misha nursed her glass and drew a deep breath with every sip as the acidic wine stung the back of her throat.

And then it happened. He was midsentence

when he suddenly barfed all over the table and the teak flooring. Misha had no idea where that came from. He was talking one moment and puking the next. As simple as that. As the captain rushed in to assist, Misha wished she was invisible or could be teleported to someplace else. Even the loo, the Polo Lounge had nice loos, they even had a pink couch in it! Since teleportation was not an option she excused herself and walked over to the restroom, carefully avoiding any physical contact with him. Puke on pink was a total fashion no-no.

Once in the restroom, she leaned against the counter and started practicing her stress-busting breathing techniques. It was in between breaths that she seriously contemplated running away. A look at her watch confirmed the dreary fact that public transport at this time, and in this outfit, would make for tomorrow's episode on one of those scary crime shows like *Hoshiyaar*. So Misha picked up the pieces of her scattered pride and returned to find that their table had been relocated to the corner. This time she did not argue and actually felt her eyes welling with tears of gratitude.

Samir returned from the restroom looking surprisingly sober and unrepentant. "I've been on the wagon the last couple of months. I think we should leave, this place is dull." There was no apology in it.

"Let's have a smoke and then leave." Misha stood her ground. She didn't want to make it appear as if she was running away out of embarrassment. She also needed to digest this latest "on the wagon" bit and meditate on the different ways to hurt Ric.

"Sure." Samir shrugged nonchalantly.

They sat in silence as Misha took long drags of her cigarette in an effort to appear calm. Meanwhile, Samir developed some sort of weird tic thingy and kept grabbing his ear every now and then, much like a mangy dog. He probably mistook it for a fly, the way he kept going at it.

As his attempts to grab his ear grew more aggressive, Misha decided it was time to bolt. She finally put out her half-smoked cigarette. "Shouldn't we leave them a tip?"

"For these guys? This place sucks. Let's get out of here," he said, stomping off. Misha rummaged through her purse and found two hundred-rupee notes. She dropped them on the table and caught the disdainful look on the captain's face. Her heels clicked noisily on the wooden floor as she went after Samir. "The flamingo has finally left the building." Someone sniggered. Misha did not bother to see who it was.

But the night was still young in Samir's book. It was as if all that puking had given him a second wind. "Let's go home," he said suggestively.

As they waited for the car at the main porch, Misha spotted a couple of familiar faces from the Polo Club. Redemption at last. And then it emerged, riding out of the darkness, a burgundy Maruti van, looking completely battered, as if fresh out of a wreck. All it needed was a ride off a cliff to put it out of its rattling misery. Samir strode toward it with almost too proprietorial a manner and force-fullly pried open the door. He got in without further ado and waited for Misha to follow suit. Misha scrambled onboard trying to adopt an I-so-don't-belong-in-this demeanor. It took two attempts to finally close the door, and even the lofty mustachioed doorman didn't come to help. She was glad not to be behind the driver's seat because she knew that her face was like thunder, and she couldn't be bothered with worrying about frown lines.

"Quite the story of the chariot turning into the pumpkin," Misha said, her tone acidic as she gazed straight ahead.

"Actually, the Merc is Dad's car. He gets in tonight, so it's gone to the airport to pick him up. If he knew I took it, I'd be dead meat." He flashed another of his toothy grins.

Misha's mind shot into the future: Her in-laws cruised in the Mercedes, wining and dining at the fanciest of places, while she lived off coupons. The only difference from her old life would be the addition of the word *free* to her vocabulary.

"I need to get home. I have an early start tomorrow."

"Come on, don't be a bore. Let's go to my place for a drink."

"Look, I think you need to get back on the wagon and I need to get home. I mean it."

"Nah . . . I know you want to come with me."

Ughh . . . that smile again. It was about all Misha could take. She pushed open the door with all her might while the van was still in motion.

Samir finally got the message. "Are you f——g crazy!" he thundered. "You chicks nowadays are psycho."

But it achieved the desired purpose. Samir dropped Misha off outside her house and drove away into the night. She stumbled into her apartment as Mrs. Mukherjee, her nosy neighbor, tut-tutted with a look of disdain splashed across her face. Right, some more grist for the neighborhood gossip mill. Misha sighed as she kicked off her stilettos. And then her attention was seized by something truly catastrophic.

Was that puke on her precious right heel?

So You Want to Be a Princess?

I tuck in an errant fold of my sari and crack open the mammoth hand-over register, the one nonautomated yet deeply pervasive influence in my life. I kick-start the day by reading the misdeeds of the past evening and planning all the recovery operations I will have to carry out. Here's how it works. Anyone can screw up with any guest anywhere in the hotel; the only commonality is my involvement. That is, I have to wipe up the mess. It comes with the territory of being a guest relations manager: I have to manage the relationship between the hotel and the guest, and the diversity and range of these relationships is unbelievable.

I am grateful to note that there are only three screwups today. One delayed breakfast order, one reported sighting of a lizard in the room, and a laundry disaster—a hole burned through a shirt. I close the book and am already ticking off the options in my head as I walk across to the concierge desk to pick up a printout of the VIP arrivals for the day: apologize for the delayed breakfast, maybe with wine and flowers; lizard—definitely rope in Housekeeping and get the room fumigated, maybe a room upgrade. The laundry disaster is a little more complicated. We will have to buy the guest a new shirt; hopefully it won't be some impossibly quaint brand.

I look at the arrivals list and snap out of my lazy perusal. My ass is grass! How did I forget that a member of the board is checking in with some inter-national guests, and we have to provide the Grand Orchid Welcome—our signature welcome. They're due to arrive in forty-five minutes, how did I forget! I moan. We charge fifty dollars a pop for this custom-designed welcome, replete with marigold garlands and Dom Pérignon for a welcome drink.

After that, the day disintegrates into one crazy rush. But this is normal, I remind myself as I dash off to the florist yet again to check on the status of the garlands.

As I am trying to get the flowers done, a princess from one of the Gulf countries decides to check in unannounced. "Unannounced" is a misleading term. Let me just say that she makes a grand en-trance into the main lobby, without prior reserva-tion. She sweeps in with her entourage comprised of a eunuch, a manager, and three minders. As the minders stand in quiet attendance of her vintage Vuitton luggage, the princess, sheathed in black with only twinkling eyes in view, goes across to the black leather single-seater and sits down.

"The princess . . ." the manager begins, towering over my boss, "would like a room, the best one you have."

For once, the boss's immaculately gelled hair looks like it's about to stand upright. "The Presidential Suite, sir, the charges are . . ."

"Please, it's not necessary to discuss that right now." The manager waves an imperious hand in my boss's face, clearly indicating that etiquette has been breached. "Give us the key, she must rest. I will take care of the registration details. And one more thing." My boss practically falls over the counter in conspiratorial anticipation. "Only ladies, please, to attend to her."

D.P.G., obviously overwhelmed by his regal guest, does something quite out of character. He snaps his fingers and calls out to me. "Aisha!"

Oh my God, I so cannot believe this! Did the classless little ass just *snap* his fingers at me? I stand my ground and refuse to budge, and then he calls my name one more time, the irritation in his voice now audible.

I force myself into action with a smile. "Yes, sir?"

"Please take the key to the Presidential Suite." He pauses, beside himself with glee at the fat killing. "And escort the princess," he finishes in a whisper.

"Of course," I reply with a tight smile.

And thus, my life changes for the next seventy-two hours. Having finally found a use for me, the boss runs around, probably like Madame Curie did when she discovered radium. After several months of trying to marginalize me, he has no option but to trust me and put me in charge. I must say, I quite enjoy all the responsibility, though I know it's only come my way because the princess requires women to attend to her, from the butler to all those in Housekeeping. Frankly, if my boss thought he could get away with it, he would wear a burka and do it all himself.

I escort the princess to her suite, and the moment she steps in, she throws off her burka. Under her sheath of the blackest black is an outfit that would shame the most audacious fashionistas. Dressed in a bright purple Juicy Couture tracksuit, with the word *juicy* implanted in an arch on her behind, she walks about the suite, inspecting each room.

"You have bidet, no?" she asks, sinking into the bed. Frette linen adorns the sixteen-inch-thick mattress.

"Yes, we do."

"Good." She smiles as she undoes the bed cover and runs a finger down the soft fabric as if to check that it actually has a thread count of one thousand. "Very beautiful room, little Art Deco, but beautiful."

I look around the suite and know just what she means. The room isn't spilling over with opulence, but that's probably why I like it, and maybe that's what makes it different for her.

Princess Fatima is to stay until Friday and I am on call around the clock until her departure. My routine is all topsy-turvy. I come in at noon and stay till about 1 A.M. Arabs on holiday eat very late and rise even later, so my working hours have to mirror hers.

On the first evening I ask for her dinner order and politely present the menu. Without bothering to read it, she runs a lazy finger down one side of the menu and stops after twelve entrées. I look at the eunuch, who nods in approval. I get the message. It is too trivial an issue to bother her with. From then on, I run all her food requirements past my eager boss, who has taken on the avatar of Doberman Pinscher, standing guard outside her suite.

"How is the princess today?" he asks with pathetic obsequiousness each time I go in or out.

"Very well, sir," I respond, "but she needs some extra towels." And off he runs to Housekeeping, to personally ensure that the princess gets the Orchid's fluffiest and whitest. He harasses Housekeeping to make sure that the towels show 85 percent on the reflectometer (a machine used to determine whiteness). He doesn't seem to realize that the younger royals, mostly raised and educated in the West— London, in Princess Fatima's case—are usually quite laid-back and egalitarian in their behavior.

Princess Fatima herself is a "zero fuss" lady and her requirements are simple—for a princess, that is. She requires a hairstylist and manicurist on standby. Fruits, cheeses, and a salad buffet—fresh and regularly replenished—are at hand in the dining room, in case she wants a nibble. And one of the rooms in the suite has been converted into a massage room for her daily Swedish rubdown with coconut cream.

The princess is in town to trousseau-shop for jewelry. So we go about arranging for the best jewelers in town to meet with her. The jewelers come in their starched safari suits with silver hard-top briefcases in hand, waiting their turn to be ushered in, each assessing the others and the size of their briefcases. But her meetings with them are fleeting and superficial, albeit profitable. It is obvious to me that she has no real interest in the jewelry. She doesn't utter a word, just points and nods, and thus a sale is made.

"They come from far and wait, it would be rude to send them away empty-handed, no?" she says with refreshing simplicity.

She leaves her suite only after dinner and arrangements have to be made according to her mood. While I go in to determine the gastronomic flirtation of the day, my boss waits outside for directives. Sometimes the wait is for five minutes and sometimes it is for an hour. Most times I know exactly what she wants, as I am doing the suggesting, but I keep him waiting anyway. I usually step out for barely a minute and say, "She'd like to use a Mercedes and go to the Crescent." And he dashes off to make the arrangements. I live vicariously through the princess. I feel like the Queen of Sheba. Sometimes I am tempted to ask for something ridiculous, like male belly dancers, but of course I don't. I still need the job.

But I do manage to get back at old D.P. when I stick my head out of the door and do the unthinkable. I snap my fingers at him. He is a few feet away and gives me a look of utter shock and displeasure. "She's asleep," I whisper sotto voce, "and she needs the Mercedes again tonight." Before he can respond, I shut the door in his face without so much as an apology, a snapshot of his cloudy expression embedded in my brain.

In the evenings, before dinner, the room is a flurry of activity as the princess commences her toilette and puts on her face. Her makeup is dramatic, and she chooses to do it herself while she sips Arabic-style tea. Personally, I feel she looks far more beautiful without all that makeup, softer and fresher. Bakhoor, the Arabic incense, fills the room with smoke as she holds it under her arms, letting the fragrance permeate her skin. I worry about the smoke alarm and the sensitive sprinkler system it might trigger. Her toilette is complete with a final spray of a Parisian perfume designed especially for her. It is called PHAT as in Pretty, Hot, And Tempting, and also short for Fatima. "Her Highness has many admirers in Paris," the eunuch informs me proudly.

I am fascinated by this ringside view of a veiled culture; the blend of ethnic and Western traits is charming. What alarms me, though, is her proclivity for alcohol, tequila in particular, which brings me to the more intimate aspect of her visit—her lover, an older Arab gentleman who has been given an adjoining room.

The eunuch is the go-between, although I am well aware of the situation. I am told that her friend is not to pay for anything, and if he does, she will be most upset. I communicate this directive to my boss, who rushes off in a frenzy to send out a group page to the entire hotel. It could be done later, but my boss is a bit of a drama queen, plus he wants the prestige of being in close proximity with a VVVIP guest. Suddenly, everyone is listening to him, probably for the first time in his working life.

The princess and I fall into a comfortable pattern soon enough. She rises at around 2 P.M. and has her brunch served with Marlboro Lights at about three. Her meetings with the jewelers begin soon after. Around 7 P.M., her toilette commences, along with her first drink for the evening. She then goes down to one of the restaurants for dinner, where I assume she drinks some more before returning to the suite and resuming the binge till about 5 A.M. This is her routine and so it becomes mine, without the booze, unfortunately.

The happy pattern is broken on Thursday, the day before she is to depart, when she gets into a vicious fight with her lover. It is in Arabic, and I cannot tell what the row is about, but emotions don't always need the language of words. My suspicions are confirmed when the gentleman storms into his room and begins packing his bags. He speaks to me for the first time in a clipped and refined accent, asking for a car to be arranged to take him to the airport. When he leaves without saying good-bye to the princess, she dissolves into tears with her head on the eunuch's lap. The eunuch runs his hand lovingly through her hair and coos softly in her ears. I know that tonight there will be no need for dinner or the favored Mercedes. I turn away helplessly, unable to do anything. Given the opportunity, I would gladly show her a night out in town; she looks like she needs it.

That day, I check on the princess one last time before I leave work. It is very late and she is as I left her, except that now she sits alone, cradling her miniature tequila and crying her heart out. She does not even notice my discreet presence as I draw the curtains and set the AC to her preferred nighttime temperature. I look at her one last time and see not a princess but a girl with a broken heart, without any friends to hold her up.

Emancipation of Me

*T*he experience with Samir makes Misha swear off men—for about two weeks. She says she is on a "loser's streak." Gamblers have losing streaks, and single women who date have a loser's streak: Misha has been on a loser's streak ever since she started dating. She is the first to admit that she seems to be a magnet for the moochers. This leads her to the wise deduction that her karma needs to be worked on, as does her aura. She is clearly not exuding the right light to attract the right man. You didn't know it was as simple as that, did you? Just radiate the right hue of pink or red light, and you're all set. I think I offended her by suggesting that the easiest solution would be for her to invest in a strobe light for her boudoir. But having said that, I find myself becoming a reluctant believer; my loveless state seems to be leading me in strange directions.

Misha says that we have to commence by exonerating ourselves of past misdeeds. Once our pores are cleansed, we can once again hope to exude the positive energy, and yeah, the right colors, which are currently clogged by our sins.

We decide to drop men altogether and empower ourselves with a havan.

As planned, Nic, Ric, Anushka, and I show up at Misha's place and waste no time in organizing ourselves on the rooftop.

Tip number one for anyone attempting to host a havan: No, you don't need a pandit, you only need to know how to start a fire. The five of us have absolutely no idea how to begin. The closest we've come to lighting anything is a candle or a ciggie, or a ciggie with a candle, and once even a candle with a ciggie—but don't try this at home. It's not dangerous or anything, it's just a bloody waste of time. So this then is the limited range of our pyrotechnic skills, and of course, we run from anything that resembles a gas stove.

"We need a man," Misha announces after half an hour of blowing at some sticks. The four of us look up at her in disappointment. She has already given up on her vow. This is not an auspicious start. Just when you feel free and empowered, life reminds you that you need a man. "I mean a watchman, guys!" Misha laughs. Of course! These are the only men in our urban jungle who still light fires.

Nic and Misha go off in search of a suitable boy and return in fifteen minutes. A hundred bucks later, we have a blazing fire. As at all our parties, the bar is overstocked with alcohol and skimpy on the food. We give the term *liquid diet* a new twist.

As we laze around the fire, drinking and discussing Misha's unfortunate date, Nic suggests we play Truth or Dare. Yes, that is one of the things that has survived high school and prospered with our terrible taste in men.

"Shush," Misha slurs as we all crowd around a just-emptied bottle of wine. "Snoopy Mrs. Mukherjee is probably out there spying on us." Truer words were never spoken, as we are doomed to find out not much later.

A year ago we were involved in a nasty run-in with Mrs. Mukherjee, the occasion being a rather loud party we had on the rooftop. Ever since, she has been keeping tabs on Misha. In all fairness, though, Misha's nocturnal behavior would keep anybody interested. The trouble is that Mrs. Mukherjee has a very fixed notion of bhadralok and Misha just doesn't cut it. It has become her life's ambition now to get Misha evicted.

Bhadralok—the wonderful term for "gentry" in the eastern state where Mrs. Mukherjee hailed from. Being "bhadro" was an often repeated rejoinder in her arsenal of accepting or dismissing people into the neighborhood committee. We all know where Misha fell on that side of the divide.

Ric gives the bottle a spin and it stops at Misha. "So . . . is it truth or dare?" he inquires.

"Well, since we are saying good-bye to past loves, it's going to be truth. I have a confession to make." We all lean forward in anticipation. "Aisha, remember that model guy you dated briefly?" Of course I remember! We were at this fashion show and there he was, all shirtless and bronzed with rippling muscles. As was our norm when confronted with a unanimously hot man, we put into practice the equal-opportunity routine and I triumphed fair and square. We dated for about two months and then sort of drifted apart. Nothing dramatic. He traveled a lot and the calls eventually dried up. That was okay, 'cuz we never really had much conversation anyway.

"Yeah, what about him?"

"I sort of had an encounter with him after you guys split up," Misha says cautiously.

"He isn't ET. What do you mean by 'encounter'?"

"I . . . ran into him at a club. . . . You know alcohol, music, but I didn't sleep with him," Misha defends herself.

The model guy was not a great love, but he was still my trophy boyfriend. And now everyone is looking at me, waiting for a response or, even better, a catfight, but they are going to be disappointed. "Well, no big deal really. It was over between us and he was fair game."

"Since you're taking it so well," Nic chimes in, "I

sort of hooked up with him too." This is most surprising. "I think he thought I was a fashion designer." The guy was not a bright spark, but there was no need to lead him on. Reading my mind, Nic goes on to state, "I did tell him I was an interior designer. I guess it didn't register."

I can believe that. Very little had *registered* with model boy. Unable to entirely curb that teeny-weeny bubble of envy, I blurt out, "So, just how many of you hooked up with him?" Anushka and Ric glance around uncomfortably. Their silence is my answer. "Come on, guys, what was he, the holy Ganges that everyone had to take a dip?" I say, unsure if there is more to follow.

My friends hesitate to make eye contact and I enjoy their discomfiture, but then my ill-timed sense of humor takes over, and I double up with unbridled laughter. The awkward moment passes, and we decide to get into the havan experience.

We make little speeches that we punctuate with shots of tequila. Then Ric says that since the fire is such an integral part of the experience, it is not to be deprived of Mexico's national drink. You know the deal with *tequi-la*, it can sometimes *kill-ya*? Well, it kills the party in no time at all. We have a blazing fire and the flames and our spirits soar in tandem. We nearly don't hear the sirens that herald the arrival of the fire truck. And then a major drama unfolds.

As we rush to the edge and peer over the parapet, we see the fire truck pull in and a circle of about eight people looking straight up at us. "Ooh, how exciting!" squeals Ric. "Is a fireman going to come up a ladder and rescue us?"

"What you need is a good hose-down," Nic comments drily.

"Cold water doesn't quite work with me, darling." Ric smirks back.

"Shit," Misha slurs, waving vigorously with both hands, "I can see Mrs. Mukherjee. . . . Hello, Mrs. Mukherjee, we're okay." To the audience below, it looks like we are calling for help. Immediately, loud shouting ensues, with more people rushing to join the crowd. In thirty seconds, there is a gathering of about twelve people below.

"Relax, no one can hear us. Douse the fire, you two," Nic says, looking at the very drunk Misha and Ric. "Anushka, turn off the music. Someone help her get rid of the booze!"

I am glad Nic is taking charge, as I have gone into freeze mode once again. "Aisha, let's head down there and handle this." Nic grabs me by the hand. It takes us twenty minutes to explain the commotion. Mrs. Mukherjee is the hardest to pacify, and insists on going upstairs to gauge the extent of the damage for herself.

"Mr. Pathak," she thunders to a small mouse of a man, "come and see what they're up to. I am sick of this girl!"

Mr. Pathak, obedient as a poodle, nods his head in disdainful agreement, and Mrs. Mukherjee, with her lackey in tow, launches her ample derriere up the stairway with Nic and me following closely behind.

"One more reason why I'm gay," he whispers, indicating the expanse of her posterior. I give him a little whack on the butt in response. As Nic mock yelps, Mrs. Mukherjee turns around suspiciously. We are definitely not making a good impression.

"Your friend, what job does she have? She has no timing...going and coming when she wants..." Mrs. Mukherjee asks by means of impolite conversation.

Misha actually works as an insurance adviser. She comes from a well-to-do family in Bhatinda, and works if and when she has a client or when her liaison officer at the insurance company pleads with her. Bade Papaji—Big Poppa, the family patriarch—got her the job and she doesn't want any negative feedback finding its way to Bhatinda. It would mean a quick trip home and the end of freedom. For Misha, this job in Delhi means a release from the shackles of small-town living and gidda soirées, and not the money or career prospects it offers. In the north of India women engage in not-always-friendly dance-a-thons involving graceful communal movements in dizzying circles. Misha quite naturally at nearly thirty and having left the small confines of Bhatinda had rightfully decided that she had danced her last dizzying gidda. She has no fixed routine as she picks her clients more often than they choose her. Besides, her parents are happier with her away. They don't have to keep explaining why their kudi is still not married. Misha herself is circumspect about her roots. The big city has tutored her well, and she always answers any question about where she grew up with a breezy "up north."

"She's evil," Nic mouths. I silently concur. Misha has met her match in Mrs. Mukherjee.

"This is a decent colony." The old cow is bristling. "There are young children here. TV is bad enough, now they also have real-life examples!" The way she is speaking, you'd think Misha does nude pilates out in the open every morning. Reality TV is big in India, but we offer free entertainment for all to see, I think cheekily.

We finally reach the terrace after what seems an eternity. An eerily normal sight greets us—no bottles of alcohol in view, the fire all put out. Misha and Ric sit close together, quite obviously propping each other up, and Anushka is standing with a bottle of Coke in her hand. Mrs. Mukherjee's disappointment is palpable. She hoped to find a flaming orgy, preferably with alcohol, and if possible, some hash thrown in. She probably rehearsed her outraged civilian call to the up-to-the-minute news channel Aaj Tak about the *ashleel* (vulgar) youth of today.

"It looks okay to me, Mrs. Mukherjee," Mr. Pathak dares to whisper.

"Hmph, they are very clever, especially this one," she says, pointing to Misha. "I will take care of this situation one day. Just remember, I have my eye on you. This girl, I tell you ..." She whirls around and huffs down the stairs like a beleaguered steam engine. Mr. Pathak gives us a reproachful sniffle and shuffles after her.

"Congratulations, Mish, she called you a girl." Ric nudges Misha and she topples over.

"And as of today, you have a neighborhood watch solely dedicated to your movements," Anushka adds.

Champagne Tastes on a
Beer Budget

*O*h, dear, you see the same people everywhere...."
Ric moans as we walk into the Ritz Continental for
our Sunday brunch.

Anuj's exit from our life did not dull our taste
for chicken tikka or the Sunday brunch. Anushka
likens our enthusiasm for chicken tikka to our collective romantic lives. She calls it the "Jerk Chicken
Syndrome," similar to the famous Jamaican jerk
chicken served at the Orchid. Our taste in food, she
says, with its unwavering fondness for chicken
tikka, is like our taste in men—in our case, the jerk
variety.

To get one of "the tables" at a Sunday brunch,
you have to make a reservation at least seven days in
advance. This time, however, I called in a favor with
a contact at the hotel.

"I was here last week and the place was full of screaming little brats," Nic grumbles, echoing his partner's dissatisfaction with the choice of venue.

"We have a table outdoors, Nic," I say, quickly changing the subject and hopefully the mood; these two are contagious.

My contact has kept his word and we are ushered to one of the tables. We are in interesting company. There is a society queen in one corner, with her equally regal designer friend. A large table of dinks commands attention; it looks like some celebration is under way as a bottle of bubbly is being popped open. One of the tables is occupied by a large group of Germans; there is a lot of laughter and abundant beer. And then there are the five of us, eclectic and fabulous.

"Ooh, can you say 'sauerkraut'?" Ric exclaims, taking in one rather delightful German specimen.

"Oh please. He's sitting with his wife," Misha exclaims as she grabs the chair with the best view of the Germans.

"Yeah, right. He is as straight as a pretzel." Ric waves her aside.

Nic smiles indulgently, and I have to admire his patience. Ric and he have been partners now for five years and are frankly teetering on the edge of domesticity. Rumor has it that they met at a party somewhere. Both of them had a little too much to drink. It was *lush* at first sight. One lush discovering another. A few wine and cheese evenings led to a promise to do every wine trail from South Africa to Bordeaux together. And the rest is history. Although I have heard from unconfirmed sources that the first meeting was rather *au naturel,* à la George Michael, at Nehru Gardens or somewhere.

"Hi, Aisha, where have you been?"

I turn around to see my friend Vishal. "I should ask you that. You disappeared after your wedding!" I exclaim, getting up to give him a hug.

"I know. It's been very hectic with all the traveling and stuff. " His eyes settle on Anushka as she excuses herself to go to the buffet.

"Well, where's the wife?"

"In Europe . . . Work stuff." His eyes dart about. I hate speaking to such people; it's as if they are never in the moment, and every interaction is reduced to an exchange of words with little or no relevance.

I have known Vishal for years. We were very good friends, technically still are, but ever since he got married, things have changed. All right, let me be honest here, everything has changed. The Maruti 800 was traded in for a Ford Endeavour, the Titan for a Tag Heuer, the DDA apartment for a farmhouse, the Nike sneakers for Gucci loafers. I think you get the drift.

As equality between the sexes becomes more the norm, some situations go unisex. Like PMS. I can't prove it scientifically, but I swear my boss suffers from it routinely; in fact, more routinely than I do. And then, there's the new male version of the gold digger, once synonymous with the female of the species.

The qualifications of the male gold digger are as follows: He is good-looking, well educated, suave, sophisticated, with certain honorable pursuits such as golf and polo, and usually in the process of setting up a "startup" venture. The winning characteristic, however, is his ability to pursue a girl assiduously. He is willing to go to great lengths to prove his love prior to circling the fire.

Which is exactly what Vishal did. What is admirable about him is that throughout his courtship of Rohini, he was clear about his intentions, but only with his closest friends, of course. "Look, I can't work for anyone and I don't have the cash to start anything, so Rohini's my ticket, man" was his consistent refrain. I, his confidante, was naturally dropped soon after the wedding.

"So, what's been happening with you?"

"The usual . . . Wife's away traveling," he says, not sounding in the least bit perturbed. Since I asked about him, not his wife, I guess he derives a large part of his identity from her. Rohini runs a successful garment export business, with buyers all over the world, from Italy to Singapore.

"I was wondering if you wanted to meet up sometime?" he asks.

"Sure." I agree impulsively.

"Great, I'll call you." He winks at me and walks away.

"Who was that dreamboat?" Misha inquires.

"An ex-colleague from work. He got married and left."

"So he quit his job?" Misha exclaims. "Hmm . . . I've heard of women quitting their jobs after getting married, but a man? How very, err . . ."

". . . Metrosexual," Ric contributes.

As I wait for my Caesar salad at the live counter, I hear another familiar voice behind me. This one sends a tingle down my spine.

"Of all the salad counters, in all the hotels, in all the world, she walks into mine."

I turn around and smile. "*Casablanca*, 1942, my favorite movie."

"Mine too. I hope you don't mind my spoofing it then." Karan Verma smiles back at me. I have rehearsed my next social encounter with him a million times over in my mind, and it was nothing like this. But here I am, grinning like an idiot. "I'm sick of the same hotel food, no offense." He is at his most charming.

"Hey, I just work there, I don't cook the food." I shrug and am about to move on when Misha suddenly appears.

"Hi there." She is positively salivating. "We nearly met the other night. I'm Aisha's friend, Misha."

"Hi, of course I remember." He winks.

"Why don't you join us for lunch?"

"I'm sure . . . umm . . . Mr. Verma has company. . . ." I butt in helplessly.

"Karan," he corrects. "Actually, I'm alone. I just hopped across for a bite. I'd love to join you, thanks," he agrees affably. "Besides, I'd love to meet your husband," he whispers to me as Misha walks on ahead.

And just like that, I lose my appetite. I walk back grimly to the table I procured with such difficulty and watch as Karan Verma happily sandwiches himself between an adoring Misha and an enraptured Ric. He is holding up rather well despite the inquisition that has already begun. So here's the brief: He works in New York for Goldman Sachs as a financial analyst. He has been deployed here for two years to set up their office in Delhi. He is in the process of finding an apartment but is taking his own sweet time because the idea of doing his own laundry is mortifying. *Cute.*

"He's nice," Anushka whispers to me. The worst thing about close friends is that they always seem to know your little *lurve* secret even before you acknowledge it to yourself, and they can't help but announce it in the presence of the guy. Not subtly, either. It's usually done with a nudge or some overt eye action.

"Can we talk about this later, please?" I say tersely.

Anushka gives me an annoyed look and turns her attention to Nic.

I go back to staring at my virginal Caesar salad with no one to talk to at a table of six. As I play four corners with the romaine lettuce, I sneak a sly glance at Karan. He is wearing a white V-neck shirt and beige drawstring linen trousers. The look is very casual chic. I suddenly feel overdressed in my carefully put-together outfit. This is terrible. Why is it that whenever I really like someone, I suddenly feel like I am all wrong, totally inadequate, and the other person is ever so perfect?

"So, Aisha, your job must be quite interesting?" Karan asks me out of the blue.

"Her job is very glamorous and she meets all these interesting people, right, Aisha?" Anushka jumps in. Now this tactic is a close second to the nudge and girly giggle. It's when your friends shamelessly try to plug you in front of a new love interest.

"I'm sure." Karan smiles politely. "I always find her hopelessly busy."

"It's seasonal, really. Right now, with all the holidays, it's a bit dull. It can get a lot busier," I say mechanically.

"And is your husband also in the hotel business?"

Five pairs of eyes turn on me.

"I'm . . ."

"Oh, she's *divorced* now, right, honey?" Ric grins.

"Oh, *that* explains things." Karan raises an eyebrow at me.

"Explains what?" Anushka asks.

"The lurking."

"The what?" Anushka prods.

"I don't lurk. This is preposterous!" I fume, all self-righteous.

Unfortunately, Misha chooses that moment to join in. "Yeah, Aisha doesn't lurk. So what if she saw you naked? No big deal."

Damn, I forgot I told her.

"Oh, I heard it was a real 'big' deal," Ric chimes in.

Clearly, I told Ric as well. The thing with secrets and me is that I usually can't remember who I've shared them with, especially when I'm under the influence.

"I thought you didn't get a good look," Misha accuses me crossly.

There is a long silence as we all direct our eyes at the food.

But then Misha's innate curiosity takes over and she presses Karan for more information. "So, where's your family? Are they joining you here?"

"Well, I'm single"—big collective sigh from Misha, Ric, and, yes, myself—"my parents live in San Francisco and my sister is a doctor who also lives in California. She's married with two kids."

"San Francisco is the gay capital of the world, at least of the U.S.," Ric says brightly.

"I wouldn't really know about that. I went to college in Atlanta."

Just then Karan's mobile rings and he excuses himself.

"Why did you say I'm divorced?" I whisper angrily to Ric the moment Karan is out of earshot.

Ric does not answer my question. He is too busy staring at Karan's retreating figure. "He is *so* gay. I just knew it. My gaydar never fails," Ric exclaims, leaning forward excitedly. More than a gaydar, Ric has a compass, one that always settles on the best-looking man in a five-kilometer radius.

"Everyone's gay in your world, Ric!" Misha shoots back.

"Oh, but they are, darling. They just don't know it yet." Ric smiles, crossing his arms over his chest.

Karan returns and Nic turns to him immediately. "We were wondering about your sexual preference."

I choke on my wine. I am truly traumatized at this point. How can my friends do this to me? I want to run and never look back. Or, better still, I wish that the Carrara marble flooring would swallow me up at the press of a button in true Bollywood style.

"I'm straight. I have a cousin who's gay; we grew up together, so he keeps me updated," Karan says casually as though he is asked this question all the time.

"You know, there is this whole debate over nature versus nurture. Some people believe your sexual preference is a genetic thing. . . ." Ric insists on taking the awkward conversation further.

"Oh, give it up, Ric." Misha sighs.

"Anyhow, let me know if your cousin is visiting anytime soon. That's if he looks like you." Ric winks, full of gayful banter. Karan grins gamely as I drink my wine in one quick gulp—anything to dull the pain.

"Oh, shut up, Ric. And Aisha's never been

married. She's single and totally *available*." Nic has reached his level of endurance.

I clamp my teeth on the champagne flute and nearly end up with a chunk of glass in my mouth, albeit of the finest lead crystal.

The Hunk and the Frump

*V*ishal telephones early the next day to confirm our date. As I dress for the evening, Mama Bhatia calls. She wastes no time in telling me just how upset she is about my recent run-in with Nina Maasi. Nina Maasi and Mama Bhatia could well enter the *Guinness* book for the longest-running feud—read sibling rivalry. My marriage, or rather the man I hook, is to be the deciding factor in this war. Nina Maasi's daughters are married, so technically she is already a step ahead. But if I find the perfect match, Mama Bhatia will leap-frog to victory.

Nina Maasi, like her sister, started the conversation that day with the standard question: "So, beta, when will you give us some good news?" Usually I responded with a cute singsong, "Not this time, Maasi." But this time I was at work and preoccupied. Anyhow, I had a gazillion reasons to say, "Well, I'm pregnant." There was a stunned silence, and that was the end of that lyrical interrogation.

"Your city girl sense of humor does not appeal to everyone." Mama Bhatia is clearly cross.

"Well, she's always asking for good news, so I gave her some. Didn't want to disappoint her," I say, the irritation rising in my voice. According to my mother, whenever something is not right with me, it's because I live in the big, bad city on my own, and did not get married when I was supposed to.

"Well, I just want you to know that it's bad enough your touching thirty and remaining unmarried—where's the need to further scandalize the family?" It is another matter that I have been touching thirty since I turned twenty-five. As for scandalizing the family, I've been doing that for quite a while. I think the first time was at the age of ten at a family function. I had gathered my troup of little cousins and we sang and danced to Madonna's "Like a Virgin." I was the lead singer, of course.

The rest of the conversation consists of some heavy-duty gyaan, lecturing which is obviously supposed to change my entire worldview. When she gets on her soapbox, my mother can give Deepak Chopra a run for his money. I have told her on many occasions to patent the verbiage and sell it to mothers with latchkey kids. Perhaps burn a CD or something. That way, while the mommies are away at work, the ayah or bhaiya can pop in the CD and the mommies of the world can rest assured that their kids will not be spared maternal nagging at its best.

It could mean major money and a larger trousseau for me.

In all fairness, life has not been particularly kind to my mom. First there is me and then there is my dog. My mother hates dogs, but bowing to familial pressure, she ended up housing one. Julian is a St. Bernard, huge, furry, and very cute. One of those dogs that you see in pictures aiding rescue efforts in the Swiss Alps with a barrel of brandy around its neck. My mom agreed to keep him with the aim of mating him for puppies. One St. Bernard pup can go for as much as twenty-five thousand rupees. Only it turns out that Julian just can't get it up, so there is no way he is going to earn his keep and spawn his own little cottage industry. Between impotent dog and unmarried daughter, Mama Bhatia's social future is sealed. If she is not dodging the "When is your daughter getting married" question, it's the "Why don't you mate your dog, he'd have such cute puppies?" As though this round of questioning isn't enough, in a cruel twist of irony, the dog gets more proposals than I do. When you are as socially active as my mother, it's a tightrope walk every day.

As I get ready, I realize that I am in no mood to go out. Forcing myself into a pair of jeans—I don't remember them being so tight!—I fret over the tedious evening ahead of me. The only good thing is that Vishal loves to talk and is unlikely to notice my punitive silence.

To his credit, though, he takes me to one of those really classy piano bars, a little old-fashioned but very *Casablanca*. I am wearing jeans, so you can imagine how appropriately dressed I am. The problem is that Vishal's idea of a casual evening has obviously changed drastically, owing to his marriage. I have my faithful credit card with me, but Vishal says, "Don't worry, I'll put it down as entertainment on the wife's account. It will be a tax write-off." I hate to admit this, but I don't need any convincing to go along with that.

As we swig back the Chardonnay, courtesy of the wife's expense account, I realize for the first time that marrying for money isn't too bad really. Don't they say you must always marry above your station, at least one rung above? Considering my bank account, that won't be very hard. I decide to realign my efforts.

If you suffer from the misconception that you never get a hangover after a night of wine drinking, let me tell you, you have to be French for it to apply. And we're not even talking about the cheap stuff here.

I wake up the next morning with a headache from hell. It hurts just to move my head from one side to the other, so I lie back in bed, head cradled on the pillow and eyes staring at the ceiling. Thanks to the princess and the overtime, I have two days off. When the phone rings, my first thought is: Please let it not be the boss changing his mind and calling me in to work.

"Hello," I groan like a pig in an abattoir.

"Aisha, is that you?" It's more of a statement than a question. It's my boss.

"Yes, I just woke up. A bit of a sore throat."

"I thought you sounded different. Look, that chap in room 345 needs to go house hunting this afternoon. You have to take him. I have to attend my wife's nephew's mundan."

Wife's nephew's mundan, my ass. I know just what and who he will be attending to, and it's not a child's symbolic head-shaving ceremony. Anyway, why should I help a guest who pays three hundred and fifty dollars a night find alternative accommodation? But, of course, I have no choice. Duty calls.

Karan Verma is to pick me up in an hour. I stare at the mirror and gently touch what should have been cheekbones. But today it would take an elite expedition to find bone under the mound of flesh. My face is bloated and shapeless, the bags under my eyes further accentuating my beauty.

I know the one party hag who will have the answer to my problems.

"Ric, help! I had a bit too much vino last night and I have to meet Karan Verma, the superdude, in an hour. I'm bloated with dark circles and a headache. Not to mention that I'm completely losing it!"

"Relax," Ric drawls lazily. I can visualize him stretched out like a Persian cat on his bed of black satin, an eye mask perched on his head. "It's totally manageable." And he lists the steps to recovery. "How bad are the dark circles?"

"Terrible!"

"Will concealer work?"

"No, not this time."

"Right, no problem. Do you still have those Jackie O shades?"

"I also have the J.Lo ones," I volunteer enthusiastically.

"No, darling, you need really dark glasses, no tints. So find the Jackie O ones, and remember, even if he takes you into a cave, don't take them off."

"Well, he isn't Batman. I'm sure he doesn't plan on living in a cave," I say in a clumsy attempt at humor.

"If you want to be his Robin . . . I always thought those two had something going on. You know Batman and Robin, their bond—"

"Ric, please focus. I don't have the time here," I interrupt irritably before he launches into his thesis on homoerotic subtleties in popular culture.

"Okay, then, how's the headache?"

"It's as if I have a heartbeat in my head."

"Remember, no caffeine. Pop an aspirin but first make yourself a banana milk shake. If that's too much work, eat an apple and take an aspirin."

"Fine."

"Now, for the bloated face. Take a scarf and tie it around your head. It's sunny today, so it will pass. Wear one of those boho skirts you have with a sky-blue peasant blouse. And listen, just go all the way with the boho chic look." Ric knows the contents of my wardrobe better than I do. He has checked me into fashion rehab so many times, though I've yet to shake off my addiction to jeans and oversize tees.

"Should I carry a wicker basket with apples in it and give Grandma a call?" I say sarcastically and a tad ungratefully.

"Well, we wouldn't be having this conversation if you hadn't been such a bad girl."

"I know, darling. Thank you, as always," I say gratefully.

When I look at the final result, it is a little OTT (Over the Top). In what way, you ask? Sort of like a movie star with big sunglasses, in the wrong neighborhood, in any part of the world. But it still beats the original pumpkin-faced avatar.

The bell rings and I hastily snatch the clothes strewn about my apartment and dump them in the closet before letting Karan in. The place definitely has a morning-after look about it. If Karan is taken aback when he sees me in my shades, he is too diplomatic or too indifferent to show it. I grab my bag and scuttle him out in five minutes. We are soon on our way to the real estate office.

I never imagined that a property dealer could be smarter or more chic than myself. But Tantalizing Tanya, the real estate chick, is in her early thirties

and very well put together. You know the type. I
mean, we've all encountered these perfectly crafted
women. It's like they pick out everything—body
parts, hair tints, accents—from a catalog.

As we shake hands, she gives me a quick dismis-
sive once-over. Her reaction to me is sort of like:
"Shouldn't you be at home quietly living out your
life through one of those regressive TV soaps?"

There is also one other thing that is truly disconcerting about her: She is limp-wristed and seemingly
without any control over her hands, yet like strategically guided missiles, they manage to land, time and
again, on Karan's biceps. I take a surreptitious
glance at her hand and note the absence of a wedding
band. Chicks like her always wear a wedding band
twinned with a solitaire. This is getting worse. Not
only is she desirable, she is also available. And Karan
seems more than happy to indulge her, laughing at
her jokes and inane comments. They are completely
into each other. I could lift up my skirt and shout
"Look, no underwear!" and I don't think he would
even notice.

The two apartments she shows us are quite
lovely; in fact, one is nearly perfect. Karan also
seems quite taken with it. He is polite enough to acknowledge my presence and ask for my opinion. So I
do what any confident, honest, and secure woman
would do. I tell him that he can find something much
better in his budget. Karan doesn't say anything, but

the lease lady flashes her contact-lensed peepers at me with newfound admiration. She obviously underestimated me, but alas, it is too late. We eventually end the meeting because Tantalizing Tanya has to "do lunch" with someone. Aha, more like *do* someone. I know the type.

"How about Chinese?" Karan asks, interrupting my bitch moment.

"Okay, sounds good." Everything sounds good now.

"So, umm, how do you know Tanya?" I ask, unable to hold back the question any longer.

"Tanya is my mom's best friend's daughter," Karan replies quite matter-of-factly.

And then I have one of those profound moments of inner deliverance. There isn't a bolt of lightning or anything so dramatic, but plain as day, the whole afternoon makes sense to me. This is a setup. Tanya was hitting on Karan and Karan shamelessly used me as a repellent!

"If you don't mind, can we go to one of those local Chinese places?" Karan asks.

"Gobhi Manchurian has always been a personal favorite," I reply vaguely.

Karan grins. He is feeling nostalgic. "I really want some Indian Chinese. You know, with dollops of MSG and all. The fancier places ignore the Indian palate in the name of authenticity." Typical. He is obsessing about food, while all I can think about is my rival.

———

Karan and I enter a place called the Oriental Dragon. It quite slipped my mind that local Indian Chinese joints conform to a decor that is almost always in lurid shades of red, not to mention the minimal lighting they favor. This one too lives up to the characteristic traits of its genre—you know, red walls, paper lamps of the lowest luminance, wall-to-wall carpeting with a dragon imprint, and a faux Chinese hostess who smiles at us or perhaps at the fact that I still have my Jackie O shades on. I nearly miss a step on the way to our table, but luckily Karan preempts the mishap by grabbing my elbow.

"You know MSG is carcinogenic," I state, trying to make a last-ditch attempt at escape as I grope my way to the table.

"So is wearing dark glasses in dingy restaurants, silly," he teases. "Live a little dangerously."

Live dangerously! If he only knew! I had forgone the concealer, confident that I was never going to remove my sunglasses. It is an opportune moment when Karan excuses himself because I am desperate for some Diva Intervention.

I call Ric. "Hey, we're in one of those dingy Chinese places. I can't see a thing. Can I remove the shades?" I sound desperate even to my own ears.

"Gosh, how tacky! He took you to one of those?"

"Ric, focus! What should I do? I don't have any concealer on."

"Shortcuts, shortcuts," he muses out loud. "I still can't believe he took you there—"

"Ric!" I plead, not wanting a discourse on the ethics of cosmetology or on how terribly tacky this man is. I think it is clear to everyone that Karan harbors no romantic interest in me. His dining option for the afternoon is evidence enough; he would never bring Tanya there. So the glares can come off, right?

"Never." Ric reads my thoughts. "Don't you dare. If you take them off, then never ever call me for advice. You don't want to look like a bag lady."

"Ric, okay, thanks, I have to go." I hang up before I get suicidal and order razor blades instead of my afternoon Zinfandel. I have to wing this somehow.

Out of nowhere materializes this not-quite-authentic Chinese waiter who pulls out a large tasseled menu and presents it to me with a dramatic flourish. At least I know that it is the correct side up.

Karan returns to the table. "So have you looked at the menu? What would you like to have?" He is really going all out with the gentlemanly bullshit.

"Why don't I just let you do the ordering?" *I am as blind as a bat.*

"Are you kidding me? I'm here with a hotelier. How can I forgo your expertise? Please order something for us." I think he is enjoying himself.

For the first time, I am grateful for the long hours spent as an apprentice in a hotel. I place the order pretending to look at the menu but going entirely by memory.

As Karan makes light, unobtrusive conversation, I stress about getting through lunch with zero visibility. But Karan doesn't seem to notice how distracted I am. My hotel training comes in handy once again: I am an expert at appearing to listen intently when I am mentally not even in the vicinity.

So I sit there blind and contemplative as weird, disjointed scenarios play out in my mind. I've seen one of those kung-fu flicks where the master eats rice from a bowl blindfolded. He even expertly wipes the bowl clean right down to the last grain of rice. I wish I had invested in that kind of training. I went for karate lessons once, but that was only because Misha thought the instructor was cute.

Just then the fake Chinese waiter places a candle on the table.

"Terrible lighting. I thought we might need it." Karan winks, leaning back, his eyes sparkling with amusement.

I can't help but smile back. Damn it, I am not supposed to like him! But he's disarmed me again, though not enough to make me take off the sunglasses. Those stay firmly perched on my nose. Jackie O would have been proud.

My Bollywood Moment

*I*t's Karva Chauth tomorrow!" Misha calls when I get home that evening.

Ah, Karva Chauth, the traditional Hindu festival for married women. For this one day a year women fast for a whole day without food or water and pray for the long lives of their husbands.

"Your point being?" I reply to Misha.

"Well, aren't you going to fast?"

"I don't think so. I'm not married, remember? And I doubt I would, even if I was."

"Come on! It's auspicious. Single women do it all the time in the hope of finding a good husband, and it works. There's this lady—"

"I'm sure it does," I interrupt before Misha starts off on another success story about starvation and romantic fulfillment.

"Anushka is going to fast this year even though

she's split up. You did say that you were going to get into the whole karmic stuff with us."

I think it's the K factor that finally got to me: not karma, but Karan. It isn't like I am thinking marriage already. Let's just say I feel better disposed toward this romantic stuff. I find myself saying, "Okay, I'll do it. What's the plan?"

We are all to assemble at Misha's house because there is some little ceremony that we need to carry out in the middle of the night. The next day we are to fast and hang out with the ladies in Misha's colony. If nothing else, this will be good PR for Misha, an opportunity for her to integrate with the bhadralok in her neighborhood.

It is an admirably organized event. We contribute money and the secretary of the neighborhood ladies' association buys the sagri sweets, thali decorations, etc.

"Will they buy the sieve also?" I ask, trying to sound involved. Apart from the starvation bit, that's about all I know of the fast, courtesy of Bollywood.

I speak to my mother about my intention to keep the fast. She has not kept a single Karva Chauth in her life. It always brings out the feminist in her: "The day my husband keeps a fast for me, I'll do the same" is her refrain. This from the lady who said "I will never work. Why should I? It's my husband's responsibility to be the provider."

"Why? You're not married, this is all drama baazi," Mama Bhatia opines.

In other words we're being drama queens.

"Well, I thought that among the Punjabis, single girls keep the fast."

"That's why they have the highest divorce rate, all drama baazi only. Just like their big showy weddings. Next thing you know, the marriage is over."

"And which national survey did you pick that up from?"

The conversation ends as usual with Mama Bhatia's succinctly voiced disapproval of my lifestyle.

Anyhow, in my case, the Punjabi from Bhatinda wins out; I bunk at Misha's and set the alarm for 3:30 A.M.

"Do we have to get up this early? Let's just skip it," I say, looking at Anushka for support.

"Aisha, if we are going to do this, we have to do it right," Misha says firmly. Anushka, sly as a fox, remains mute.

We all manage to wake up on time—a major achievement—and shower. We go downstairs to assemble with the other ladies. Mrs. Mukherjee is there as well.

"Isn't she Bong? Do they fast as well?" Anushka whispers.

"I guess she's lived in the North long enough," I whisper back. She definitely unnerves us. She is also the unofficial master or, rather, mistress of ceremonies. She sort of harrumphs when she sees us but doesn't immediately denounce us for the alcohol-swigging, wild-dancing, gay-man-loving pyromaniacs we are on most days. There's something about these community thingies that makes you want to feel "decent," a part of the normal and accepted community.

Here is a breakup of the congregation. There are the first-time Karva Chauth–ers, you know, the ones who have been married for a year or less; have a streak of vermilion parting their hair to prove it; and of course a doting husband lurking in the background, who keeps the fast with them. It's really cute. Then there are the single gals. You can't tell them apart in their color-coordinated Bollywood-inspired outfits, replete with bangles and makeup. Someone show them a clock! It's four in the morning and they will have to take off all that finery in order to nap later. They have the annoyingly giggly enthusiasm of girls below the age of twenty-five. And then there's us, with the "been there, done that, but nothing worked, so might as well turn to religion" kind of desperate charm. There are also the "enthu aunties," a little mismatched in appearance because the daughters clearly got first dibs on the good stuff. They make up for it with their gaiety and sportsmanship. After all, Karva Chauth is an opportunity to display one's talents as well, with everybody showing off how well they can sing and dance on an empty stomach, and on the "sukha" (dry) fast as opposed to the "geela" fast, in which water is allowed.

Point to note: Only the young hubbies are hanging around at this unearthly hour in the morning.

I feel like a wannabe, a poseur. I have no man and no resuscitated wedding lehenga to wear. Story of my life: Every time I feel I've reached a stage where I actually fit in somewhere, I suddenly find myself in an unfamiliar place again.

So, back to this moonlit night. Everyone prays and invokes the blessings of multiple gods, just so no one feels left out, I assume. As we don't have mas-in-law, Mrs. Mukherjee gives us the sagri to eat, our sweets before the fast, and I must say it is a case of perfect casting.

After this extremely enlightening experience, we go home and pass out. I wake up later in the morning, already thirsty. As I look at my sleeping comrades, I am tempted to get a drink of water, but I restrain myself. Giving in so early would be totally pathetic. I just have to look at this as a detox thingy. People spend thousands to go to fancy places to purge themselves; I am getting to do it for free. Or so I think.

Since there isn't a ma-in-law or a husband to give us gifts, we decide to go shopping for our evening wear. There's nothing like a little retail therapy to kill all pangs, including those of hunger. I settle on a turquoise Swarovski iced–chiffon sari by Gudda—Shantanu and Nikhil to you plebes. Not very traditional, but it's not like I have the budget to match outfit to occasion each time. After this purchase, I won't be able to eat for the next month, but fortunately that fits in fabulously with the new diet I am about to embark on. Besides, this sari is definitely multipurpose and goes very well with the simple but elegant jewelry I plan to wear.

We return to our individual homes to get dressed. We are to meet the other ladies in the club-house later. The agenda is to decorate the thali, listen to stories about the legend of Karva Chauth, and dance, which I naively predict will be a contest only for the aunties and not for myself.

As expected, the new look is understated but elegant. Once I get to the venue, however, I realize that I am practically invisible. The gathering looks like a casting call for Bollywood: age and size no bar. I look like an extra or a junior artiste, although a very classy one. This time around the sari successfully conceals the flabby bits. Misha, however, in her mithai pink sari, could give any one of them a run for their money. In fact, I even see Mrs. Mukherjee giving her an appreciative once-over. She's paired her sari with a tie-up blouse à la Bollywood sex symbol Zeenat Aman and pink stilettos to match, of course.

As she taps her foot to a snappy film tune, threatening to burst into a dance, I pray for a husband for Misha to look at through that sieve next year. She is made for this stuff, and if our traditions are to withstand India's sprint toward the Western way, women like Misha have to get married.

"Oh, Lord, please don't tell me that's Swati," I groan. And bright as day, there is Swati from God's Own Country, the term used for the very beautiful state of Kefela, draped in a heavily worked baby-pink georgette sari, heading directly our way with a broad smile plastered across her face. She is twiggy thin, always has been. "Overactive metabolism," she would chirp, stuffing another carb into her mouth. I think we spent most of our time rolling our eyes at her behind her back. Therefore, it was no surprise when our friendship ended.

"Hello, ladies, it's been so long!" She has one of those annoying nasal twangs, attributed to one year of study in the U.S.

"So, how've you been?" I ask as Misha and Anushka sit with glum expressions. Swati, or Sweaty, as we call her in private, is universally disliked.

"Well, the usual—you know, work, shopping, traveling . . . getting engaged," she says, sticking out her bony hand. On it sits a beautiful pear-shaped diamond set in a platinum band, encrusted with baguettes.

Misha suddenly comes to life. She grabs Sweaty's hand and despite herself exclaims, "It's gorgeous!"

"Isn't it? It's a bit much for me, but Dhruv insisted. You know I have always had such simple tastes. But what the hell, you only get married once."

Apparently, a year or so ago, Sweaty decided that unlike us, who bemoaned our love lives, she was going to get off her ass and do something about it. She started hanging out exclusively with the dinks. For a while, she was the proverbial third wheel, but she stuck it out through the high-end grocery shopping, movie evenings, and house parties. Her persistence paid off when she was introduced to a visiting investment banker. To their credit, dinks love setting their single friends up. It's their interpretation of charity. And six months later, Swati was a glowing, happy, and bona fide Karva Chauthi.

"Congratulations." I get up to hug her. Everyone

else, though, continues with their pledge of silence. It's not like I am being fake. I do feel happy for her. Taking my cue, the others finally chime in as well.

"Thanks. Oh, Anushka, so sorry to hear about you and Anuj. You know, it's never good to rush into marriage. Anyway, I better go back to Dhruv. Do make it to the wedding; I'm going to be a December bride," she says, walking away.

What is it about single women in our age group? The day they find a man, they totally disconnect from the rest. Their single girlfriends become a burden, reminders of just how close they came to missing the boat!

My mobile chimes. It is Karan. I excuse myself just in time to escape being hoisted up to take part in the remixed version of *"Mere piya gaye rangoon,"* a popular old ditty which has a lady singing to lament her lover's departure to Rangoon.

"Hi, you just saved me from becoming an item girl."

"I'm glad. My flight's been delayed. Thought I'd chat with you. Where are you?"

"At a Karva Chauth do," I say, feeling shy and stupid.

I stand on the periphery of the balcony and speak to Karan for a really long time. He is off on a business trip to Mumbai. Fortunately for me, the dancing lasts forever as the young girls and Misha are involved in this dance-a-thon—a sort of Kathak/Bollywood face-off. It's quite hilarious, especially because the participants are so serious and competitive. I report all the moves live to Karan and he can't stop laughing. He hangs up only when his plane lifts off the tarmac. Just then a little kid runs in, declaring that the moon has been sighted. Immediately, the party breaks up, and everyone rushes out to take a look.

"I was just going to do this sliding move on my knees," says Misha, sulking, robbed of her grand finale.

"Never mind." Anushka tries to pacify her as we get our thalis together. I, for one, am thinking about my conversation with Karan and the fact that my nicotine fix is only two minutes away. I pick up my sieve and, being directionally challenged, fail miserably at trying to imitate the silly little twirl I've just watched everyone else do.

I am saved by the appearance of Ric and Nic. "Surprise," they squeal in unison as they unveil a mammoth picnic hamper. Is that a bottle of champagne? Before Mrs. Mukherjee spots them, we quickly ditch the party and relocate to Misha's roof. Ric and Nic, with the sensitivity that is the reserve of gay men, have brought a hamper with the ultimate Moët & Chandon, Boursin cheese, shepherd's pie, garlic bread, a tossed salad, and brownies, not to mention linen napkins and real silverware. Not exactly religious fare, but then we aren't great on religion either.

As we sit around sipping the bubbly under the moonlit sky, I savor the moment. Friends really are the family you choose. My mental image of the evening has Ric and Nic laughing with their arms thrown around each other, both glowing with the kind of love and commitment that's only born out of a deep sense of understanding and acceptance of oneself. Next to them is Misha, giggling and crazily vulnerable, her capacity to give love as fierce as her desire to find it. And there's Anushka, a little removed, smiling her sadder but wiser smile, and well on the path to rediscovering herself.

Love, Lies, and Lorries

*I*t's Armageddon! The most stable couple I've known through my adult life is in trouble. Nic and Ric had a roaring fight and Ric walked out. He is currently recuperating in my apartment and discussing community law like he is in California.

"Aren't you jumping the gun, Ric? It's only been two hours!" I say, hoping to console him.

"You don't get it. I've never seen him so furious. He said he could never trust me again."

"Well, he does have a point. You did breach his trust. I'm so sorry, Ric." I lean forward to take his hand.

He immediately recoils and launches into a tirade. "Your problem is that you are just so judgmental, Aisha. Not everything is black and white. And when was the last time you were in a relationship? It's not so easy!" Ric storms out, slamming the door shut.

I wait for the doorbell to ring. When it doesn't, I peek out of the window to see if he is doing his usual divaism. But this time it's different, for I see him doing something he has never done before, at least not of his own volition. I see him hail a three-wheeled auto-rickshaw and actually board it.

I have really pissed him off.

It all began one bright, sunny morning in the middle of the wedding season, the busiest time for an already busy wedding-planner team. A hyperventilating socialite and her "art consultant" daughter played the agents of doom. (By the way, have you noticed the manner in which the Page 3 culture has fostered the birth of so many new careers? Suddenly, being a lifestyle or an art consultant, or even a pashmina-shawl collector, has become a worthy way of earning a livelihood. The only real qualification required is big money to start with, and this particular socialite is loaded.)

Anyway, Nic was away in Mumbai wrapping up the arrangements for the reception to be held there, while like a sonorous chorus in a Greek tragedy, our desi Aphrodite called poor Ric incessantly. Apparently, her aesthetic sensibilities were appalled by the texture of the fabric the mandap was made of, and she wanted him to dash down with swatches of fabric to effect a change.

Ric answered every call with admirable restraint and endured her ranting with admirable resilience. Something like fifteen phone calls later, he reached for a cigarette with trembling hands and decided he had no choice but to obey. Easy enough in principle, but practically impossible in do-ability. Herein lay the problem: Ric cannot drive. What I mean is, he can drive but only on specific routes. Like the one that leads to India Gate, the memorial to fallen soldiers a stone's throw from the President's official residence, at four in the morning.

Ric is a terrible driver. To add to his dismal lack of motoring skills, he also has some other limitations, the biggest one in this case being his inability to board an auto-rickshaw. The very thought of it sends him tumbling into an anxiety attack.

"But you ride them in Thailand," I said on one occasion when he refused to come over because he didn't have a car.

"Well, those aren't autos, they're *tuk tuks*. Besides, I'm a tourist there," he explained patiently.

"Fine, then, hang a camera around your neck before getting into one," I said in exasperation.

As luck would have it, Ric's driver had chosen a rather inappropriate day to play hooky, but the wedding was big business and could not be trifled with. All options lost, Ric turned to their new second car. It was a Mini Cooper look-alike that had become such a craze. This one was in a bumblebee yellow. It was meant to be Nic and Ric's city car, but we all knew that they had bought it because it was so damn cute.

Ric made it as far as a kilometer from the house before totaling the front of the car in a smashup with a truck. A huge drama ensued with the thullas cheerfully getting involved. It was obviously Ric's fault, but he feigned whiplash and motion sickness. While the drama unfolded, he looked from the thullas to the Haryanvi lorry driver and decided to grant his ornate visiting card to the latter.

"*Shaadi-vaadi ka kaam karte ho?*" the driver asked quizzically.

"*Haan ji,*" Ric replied, rubbing his neck, frankly quite surprised that the chap could read.

"*Band vand ka bhi bandobast?*" the guy persisted.

"*Ji.*"

"*Khana vaana?*" The conversation continued.

"*Haan.*" Ric's responses were getting shorter and less respectful.

"*Daru sharu?*" Ric could not believe that his beautiful, lyrical existence had been reduced to a desi limerick.

"*Ji haan. Mujhe hospital jaana hai. Aap phone karna,*" Ric said, hoping to end the conversation.

The two distressed parties decided not to pursue the matter midstreet, much to the distress of the cops and the gathering crowd. Traffic skirmishes in our city provide such great free entertainment.

Ever the professional, Ric called the bride and her mom and said he had been in a terrible accident and had suffered a concussion. The mother of the bride was upset but understanding, and Nic was out of town anyway.

Ric then took the car to a local garage and had a quintessentially Indian jugadu (Band-Aid) job done on it. There are areas in our beautiful capital that are flooded with these two-hour mechanic messiahs. They can make your humble 800 look like a souped-up Mercedes, complete with the signage.

The car was duly returned and parked in the garage well before Nic returned that weekend. When Ric related the incident to me, I pleaded with him to tell Nic. "You know what they say, if it's done in the dark, it will come to light one day."

"It's all been taken care of," he said with the air of a seasoned criminal. He had, however, underestimated the Haryanvi lorry driver and the jugadu job.

The day of reckoning was one sunny Saturday morning a few weeks later. As Ric and Nic sat reading the morning paper and eating their croissants, there was an incessant pounding at the front door. Nic opened the door to find the lorry driver standing there with a couple of taus (rednecks) from his hometown.

"*Woh admi kahaan hai?* He hit me badly," a voice thundered in dhaba-style Hindi. As if on cue, the culprit appeared behind Nic and was spotted before he could duck behind his leafy and lovingly cared for Erica palms.

"There must be some mistake," Nic offered in chaste public-school Hindi.

"No, that's him." And Nic was unceremoniously pushed aside.

"I have no idea who these hulks are," Ric said in his most outraged voice.

But the lorry driver refused to leave. "I can show you the car that hit the lorry. It was seriously damaged and the bumper fell off." The motley crew then proceeded to the garage where he asked Nic, "Car driving okay? Suspension *ko mara.*" He was greeted with silence, but the driver was undeterred, and much like a doctor conducting a postmortem asked the next question. "The bumper came off. See?" He pointed it out to the mute audience. It looked fine to Nic and he said so. Ric breathed a sigh of relief.

Then one of the silent and evidently more aesthetically inclined taus spoke up. "Look at the paint, *peele ka alag alag rang.*" Nic peered closely at the bonnet, and sure enough, there was a clear difference in color. He promptly turned to look at Ric's face, which was also a completely different shade from the sun-kissed look he was partial to.

"Maybe it's a two-toned effect," Ric muttered uncertainly.

"So, how much do you want?" Nic said, turning to the driver calmly. The matter was settled for fifteen thousand rupees in cash. What followed was a flaming row and Ric stormed out.

Ric finds sanctuary in Misha's arms, in her apartment. They decide to shack up together till his personal situation is sorted out. The move is quite conspicuous, with the entire neighborhood and Mrs. Mukherjee figuring out that Misha has taken a man in. Interestingly, while Ric is attempting to decipher the laws of common property, Mrs. Mukherjee is contemplating the Indian Morality Act. Although neither case would be admissible in a court of law, it keeps the two mentally stimulated.

To make matters worse, if Misha and Mrs. Mukherjee have a bad karmic connection, then Ric and she definitely have some sort of a cross-connection. It commences at the break of dawn, with Mrs. Mukherjee's surya namaskar yoga exercises being interrupted by Ric's lunges to the accompaniment of his faithful boom box. Meanwhile, Misha has actually taken up an insurance job and she heads out at 9 A.M. sharp, as does Mr. Mukherjee. Every morning, when Ric and Mrs. Mukherjee bid good-bye to their respective breadwinners, Misha can't help stealing a glance at Ric and mulling over the role reversal— Ric, in a form of further protest, has ceased working and is pursuing his new profession of couch potato and online shopper.

Ric and Mrs. Mukherjee meet yet again, lured by the calls of the vegetable seller, at 11 A.M. Ric has taken over the cooking as a way of repaying Misha's hospitality. Together, they are trying out this new fad diet that requires them to abstain from all things cooked, which means that Misha is spared the mundane task of vegetable shopping, while Ric can serve up a meal without the effort of cooking.

As he conducts business with the vegetable vendor, Ric catches a glimpse of Mrs. Mukherjee's purchases. Always free with his advice, the lifestyle diva in Ric overwhelms his sense of discretion and he begins a conversation. "Why only tamatar pyaaz, Mrs. Mukherjee? For the last three days I've seen you buy only that. Your husband will run away. Get some other vegetables. There's this leafy spinach and crisp French beans . . ."

As Ric elaborates on the different vegetables and their attributes, a stunned silence emanates from the recipient of this generous advice. The vegetable vendor looks on nervously, waiting for an explosion; the term "calm before the storm" was invented for such situations. This neighborhood has been his regular beat for the last ten years, and he is not immune to Mrs. Mukherjee's wrath. She is not to be spoken to, let alone trifled with. It is common knowledge that you never tell her what vegetables to buy or at what price. While the rest of the country paid twenty-five rupees for pyaaz during the monsoons, she grudgingly made an allowance of fifteen "for the poor farmers in Maharashtra," although she was sure that the capitalist government was hoarding the onions. This is her neighborhood and no one is allowed to forget that.

Mrs. Mukherjee finally stops staring and responds to Ric. "And who will string the beans? That is the most irritating thing about *thaem*, having to string *thaem* . . ." And this, as Bogie said in *Casablanca*, is the beginning of a beautiful friendship. From then on, the relationship blossoms and it is bounteously reciprocal. Mrs. M introduces Ric to Rabindra Sangeet and he opens up for her the world of Irish coffee.

Early one morning at six-thirty, the doorbell rings and Misha rolls out of bed to answer it. "Is Ric there?" Mrs. Mukherjee is at the door, breathless.

Misha is in shock but goes to get him. "Ric,

Mrs. M is outside. I can't get evicted, please tell me everything is okay?"

"Relax, darling, we're going to work out together on the roof. I'll be there in a minute, Malini."

Malini. Now Mrs. Mukherjee even has a first name.

Then, one day, Nic realizes that business is suffering and, more important, there is no drama left in his life. He does what any man in love would do; he takes the full blame for everything and apologizes abjectly to Ric. Ric, after considering the apology for one whole day, despite knowing the answer all along, announces that he is ready to move back in.

Everything is settled. Nic stands in grateful anticipation as Ric packs his duffel bag and goes to bid his new *amiga* good-bye. You'd think he was moving cross-country or something, the amount of time it takes.

And just like that a small misunderstanding welcomes the most controlling element into a relationship—a mother-in-law, even if it is a faux or wannabe one at that.

Voodoo Lounge

*I*t is seven-thirty in the morning when Misha rings my doorbell. "Aisha, are you awake? I've been banging on your door forever," she screams.

"No, I'm talking in my sleep."

"Have you seen the paper?" She is waving it in her hand, having just picked it up from my doorstep.

"You just woke me up, remember?"

"Read the paper now, hurry."

"What happened?"

"Just read the paper," she says impatiently.

In my dreamy state, I open the paper while Misha looks on impatiently. "Yeah, so Ganguly is back on the team, what's the point?" I ask, looking at the front page.

"No, silly. Look at the supplement. Page 3," she explains.

Right, who reads the front page anymore? That's so passé! I sink into bed and open page 3. "Oh." I am looking at the photograph of a happily betrothed couple.

"Can you believe it? Rupali is engaged! This is just great; now even lesbians are getting married before us!" Misha moans. "And she has a 'brand-name' dulha!" She flops onto the bed beside me. So, what is this brand-name dulha? While the astrologer is the most required accessory these days, a brand-name dulha is definitely the most envied one. Who is he? Well, anyone with a great last name, of course! It's a priceless accessory; nothing can beat it. Names like Bachchan, Gandhi, Tendulkar, Ambani . . . You get the drift? Rupali, who was prematurely judged as being a lesbian, has bagged a brand-name dulha.

"So, I guess she's not a lesbian after all," I reply cautiously.

Frankly, I fear Misha when she gets into one of her moods, especially when jealousy rears its ugly head like when an unworthy colleague gets the promotion that you have had your heart set on. I can envision her sharpening her talons on her new metallic stilettos. "If you look close enough, you can see the ring," she continues.

I squint in an attempt to make out the rock. Frankly, I can't see anything. The resolution sucks. "Yeah, it's huge," I say, trying to make an educated guess.

"Are you kidding me? It's a *pebble*! I would have

never married anyone who gave me that, brand-name dulha or not!"

We are both staring at the picture in silent envy when the doorbell rings again. It is Anushka, looking all teary-eyed. She falls into my arms.

"What happened?" I ask, expecting the worst.

"It's just hit me, I'm getting divorced!"

"But you want this, remember? It's just paper-work. You've dealt with the baggage already."

"I know, but I never, ever thought I would grow up to be a divorcée." Like all little girls, she grew up dreaming about that perfect, life-long love.

Sometime later, Anushka confesses, "I feel like there's this nazar on me."

"Like a spell?" Misha asks. "You know, some-times I feel it too."

"Yes, I'm doing a lot of things out of character. My appetite is nonexistent, I'm accident prone... My ex-ma-in-law is really into this baba... Remember, Aisha? You met him."

"I remember going to him when I was thinking of a career switch. I'll never forget what he said. It was something like *'Beta, IAS karo, usme bahut oopari kamai hai.'*"

"No way." Misha laughs. "Join the Indian Administrative Service, there's an opportunity for lots of kickbacks? That was your path to wealth?"

"Yup, he was very worldly, this baba..."

"He was into all kinds of *jadoo tona*. But I do feel like there's something wrong with me," Anushka insists.

"Don't be a drama queen, Anushka." That's Misha, ever the realist.

"No, really . . . I feel very strange."

"It's probably just stress over the divorce." I try the practical approach as well.

"But I've been in the process of divorce for months . . . What could have happened now?"

"She has a point, Aisha. I know this lady who can remove the most powerful nazar," Misha says, getting all serious.

In India, we are equipped to handle all sorts of crises. Anxiety busters like astrologers, babas, godmen, god persons, and numerologists are our key to good mental health. They've kept us away from shrinks and therapists, unlike the rest of the world. That reminds me: I should try to pass on Karan's details to Shastriji. I am personally a little wary of the supernatural stuff. I believe the path of superstition is like this psychological vacuum cleaner with the potential to suck you into a long, dark, and winding path, where you get tossed around for a bit before being finally dumped into a dust bag. I'm being figurative here, of course, but I've been around too many superstitious relatives who have structured their entire lives around the unknown. Stuff like "Don't cut your nails at night," "Never say *oil* or *ghee* or *tel* before someone travels," etc. I could go on with this list of don'ts most Indians grow up with but will stop here as a courtesy to the more susceptible and suggestible among us.

I am on the early-morning shift and can get out only by 3 P.M., so our appointment with Roshni Ma is fixed for 5 P.M. At twenty minutes past three, Anushka and Misha shriek to a halt in front of my building. An arm quickly pulls me into the car.

"Why are you guys wearing black? You look like the death squad!"

"We have to, it's part of the whole ceremony. Don't worry, I've brought a black T-shirt for you as well," Misha says.

"This sounds more Gothic than Tantric to me."

"Shut up! This is not Tantra. Don't say things like that. Anyway, Tantra is not a bad thing. It's just the way popular culture has sensationalized it," Misha informs us.

"Misha, you're scaring me."

"We're just going for a simple nazar thingy, not vashikaran or something."

"Vashi . . . What? How do you know this crap?"

"Politicians use it all the time to make people succumb to their wishes. And I believe that among royalty in the good old days, it was totally in. Still is, I'm told."

"Oh, royalty does this stuff? Then it's definitely in," I state sarcastically.

"Stop it, you two," Anushka butts in. "Misha, how far is this place?"

"Forty minutes out of town. It's like an old abandoned mandir, a temple."

"I believe the Ramsay Brothers are location

hunting for their next horror film. You should let them know..."

It takes us longer than forty-five minutes to get there without proper directions—much like our path to romantic Nirvana—and when we pull up in front of Bappi da Dhaba for the third time, I am ready to scream.

"I'm sorry, guys. I can't remember the landmark. I think it's left from here...." Misha has a terrible sense of direction. Surprise, surprise.

"Just ask the old man sitting there," I volunteer.

"You must mean 'senior citizen,'" Misha shoots back.

"No, I mean 'geezer,' this place is creeping me out."

It's winter, so dusk is already upon us, and it's quite spooky. Thick fog begins to descend, and the only sign of civilization is this old broken-down dhaba (a diner) with a single bald lightbulb dangling from a wire.

"*Uncleji, yeh purana mandir kahan hai?*" Misha asks.

"*Jo devi wala tha?*" he croaks.

"*Haan, jahan Roshni Ma baithti hain.*"

"*Accha, woh wala...*" And he proceeds with a set of complicated directions.

As we forge ahead, Misha claims to recognize the topography. She does it in typical Misha style, full of drama and delight, like it's some sort of re-incarnation episode: "Oh it's all coming back to me now...I remember this banyan tree, and look...

there's that broken bridge!" she exclaims."This is
it!" she says, claiming victory as we finally grind to a
halt in front of a spooky old mandir right out of pre-
historic times. The mandir is a khandahar—very
decrepit.

Anushka looks a little uncertain and I seek comfort in the fact that I am not the only one with appre-
hensions.

"How much money do we have to give her?"
I ask.

"Well, usually it's fifteen hundred."

"That's one Sunday brunch!" I moan. "Does she
accept credit cards?"

"Actually, she doesn't ask for anything."

"So why do we have to give her anything? We
may offend her."

"Aisha, don't embarrass me. Just follow my
lead," Misha says firmly.

As we make our way inside, I choose to focus my
eyes on the ancient flooring. The place is probably
crawling with scorpions and snakes. Then I see that
Anushka has frozen in her tracks. I follow her gaze.
In the midst of a cloud of smoke is a woman seated
in a meditative pose in a muumuu or one of those
flowing Arabic thobe outfits, that too in shocking
pink! A sort of headband fastened around her forehead completes the very Cher look (of the seventies,
of course).

She remains in meditation with her eyes closed
as Misha signals for us to sit down. A carpet of dust
cushions my derriere when I try to settle down,

Japanese style. I've just about managed to achieve some degree of comfort in this awkward position when she opens her eyes. It has taken her fifteen long minutes. Great, we are going to be here all night. But then she gives me this look that silences my thoughts. She has piercing green feline eyes and I suddenly feel like she can slice through my thoughts.

"*Toh bacchon,* welcome, welcome," she gushes enthusiastically in Punjabi-accented Hindi, cracking the spell. Anushka and I look at each other in barely suppressed amusement. The truth is, any description I can come up with of her in that mesmeric setting would be totally inadequate. How does one describe a woman whose idea of Rodeo Drive is probably Gaffar Market? Anticlimatic, yet strangely comforting.

"*Pranam Roshni Ma.*" Misha makes the first approach.

"*Kaisa aana hua? Aur bacche, us ladke ko pakda?*" She winks.

Anushka and I both look at each other. *What brings you here? Did you manage to trap that boy?* Just how long has this relationship been going on?

"*Nahin, Roshni Ma.* I should have listened to you. I have come with my friends for nazar," Misha answers, quickly changing the topic.

"You *bacche*... never listen nowadays. Never mind, *kabhi kabhi* experience *sabse* best teacher *hota hai. Kaun ayega pehle?*"

"Misha, you go first," Anushka and I say in unison.

Roshni Ma pulls out a fan of peacock feathers and lights a dhoop, a stick of incense. She is sitting on a colorful takht, a pile of cushions, which on closer inspection looks like it belongs to the latest pastel collection of the Home Store. Misha walks across in her new tie-up stilettos encrusted with fake colored stones.

"Bahut changey joote hain," Roshni Ma says appreciatively. *Very good-looking shoes.* The compliment clearly delights Misha and she sits down with the ease of the indoctrinated.

Roshni Ma gets on with the ceremony without wasting any time. She grabs Misha's head with both hands and shakes it vigorously, similar to the manner in which tequila shots are administered in some parts of the world. I'm sure it induces the same head rush. She then proceeds to fan the dhoop with a plastic Japanese fan. You know, the kind that unfolds prettily into a tree laden with cherry blossoms. The flames begin to dance a merry flamenco and nearly singe Misha's newly acquired hair extensions. Roshni Ma then pulls out the peacock fan and starts swaying at a dizzying pace, while her hands move in tandem. She chants all the while. The ritual gains speed and intensity and peaks in an earth-shattering crescendo. It gives the impression of being extempore though it's probably carefully planned out in full detail.

"She's speaking in tongues, Anu," I say, genuinely fearful. Anushka lets out a little giggle. It is almost like Roshni Ma has heard us, because the chanting slowly subsides until it is barely audible. She finally bends down and blows into Misha's ears, then flings something over her right shoulder. The performance is over. I nearly clap, I am so involved with the scene. The entire thing has taken about five minutes but feels like thirty seconds.

Misha quietly gets up and joins us. "We need to give her ten minutes to cool down."

Ten minutes later, as though in one of those cheesy magic shows, she motions for one of us to come forward. Anushka is the next victim and the same treatment is meted out to her. As Roshni Ma does the tequila-shot maneuver, Anushka appears disoriented.

"Something's not right," I whisper to Misha.

"Shhh."

Anushka stumbles back to where we are sitting. Then I am summoned.

"*Teri shaadi toh* NRI *ladke se hogi...*" she says, suddenly raising her voice as I sit down.

"*Meri?*" I ask, turning around, thinking that perhaps she is addressing one of the other girls. Me? My wedding *toh* will be with an NRI boy?

"*Peeche mat dekh, aage hi dekh,*" she admonishes. *Don't look back, only at front.* Then she proceeds in a cheerful tone, "*Zyaada time nahin hai. Shopping-vopping shuru kar le.*" *Not much time to go. Start all your wedding shopping.* I look at my friends to see a dazed Anushka and a visibly crestfallen Misha staring back at me. I am sure that her disappointment won't last long.

My session is short, quick, and painless, except

for the head rush, and that's never a bad thing. We are finally ready to leave, our virtue and beauty protected from the evil spirits that inhabit this world and the other one as well. Misha goes over to Roshni Ma and drops the money at her feet. She indicates for us to follow suit. But Roshni Ma refuses to accept our little tokens of appreciation.

"Nahin beta, koi zaroorat nahin hai." She brushes away the money. "I want you all to be happy, that's all." I look at Misha for guidance. Her look says it all, and I drop the money at Roshni Ma's feet. But Roshni Ma insists, *"Main toh paise ko yahan hi chod doongi.* I have no use for it. Maybe a poor person will find it."

"Please, Roshni Ma . . . accept it. We are like your children. Please don't hurt our feelings," Misha says, nudging me.

"Absolutely." I nod in faux agreement.

"Chalo, if you insist . . . Praise the Goddess! *Jai mata di, bachhe."* And we all get up to leave.

I feel strangely light, I don't know why. Maybe it is the unburdening of the hard-earned cash that could have bought me a forty-five minute shiatsu massage or a Sunday brunch.

Anushka is zigzagging her way back. "What happened?" I whisper once we are out of earshot.

"While she was doing the headshaking thing, I think one of my contacts popped out."

I burst out laughing, actually more with relief than in amusement. I thought she'd gone into a trance or something.

"Misha, did you hear that? She's lost one of her

contacts," I say, offering my partially blind friend an arm.

"Guys, I don't think I can drive. Can we go back there and look for my contact?" Anushka is in a minor state of panic.

"Let's go." I take her hand in mine.

"I don't know . . ." Misha seems uncertain.

"Come on . . . she needs help."

We walk back to the mandir, but Roshni Ma is nowhere to be seen. She has vanished as though she was never there to start with. The money, as expected, is gone, so no poor person is going to get lucky today, more like the guy who sells those Bangkok jeans in Karol Bagh. The embers of the dhoop remain, but the rest of her is gone—the takht, the Home Store cushions, the peacock feather fan, everything. This is eerie; we were there just ten minutes ago, but all traces of her presence have been wiped clean. Were it not for the burning embers of the dhoop, I would wonder if she had been there at all.

"Anu, this place is empty and there is a layer of dirt on the floor. I don't think your contact is going to be found." I scour the ground for the elusive object.

"I guess you're right. One of you will need to drive, then."

"No problem, I'll drive," Misha offers.

As we reach the car, a purple Mitsubishi Lancer zooms past with the new *Chunariya* remix on full blast. Roshni Ma is behind the wheel. She zips off with a cheery wave. I wave back, utterly stunned.

"Who was that?" Anushka asks, squinting her eyes.

"Roshni Ma in her Mitsubishi Lancer. She must need to get someplace in a real hurry!"

Blended Relationships

*P*otentially the most indiscreet aspect of a social interaction is the question "So how do you know him or her?" The answer is often more difficult to comprehend than high school algebra. Here is just one example of what I've heard: "He used to be married to this girl who was friends with my husband, though they briefly dated earlier and actually introduced me to my husband...." Whew, did you get that? Never mind, in single-girl speak, the gist of it is that she's married, he's not, and they're not doing each other, so if he's cute, then he's fair game. And now, here I am, doing much the same thing. I am going out for drinks with this guy whom I've known for many years and who used to be married to my best friend; actually, they are in the process of getting a divorce and she still is my best friend. Anyhow, these are what you call blended relationships.

Anuj calls me and wants to meet up in the evening. I say that I will let him know as I have tentative plans. I am actually buying time because I need Anushka's approval. Anuj and I used to be good friends. In fact, among all of Anushka's friends, he is particularly fond of me. I was the go-between in the first year of their relationship. Of course, when Anushka and he split up, I knew very clearly where my loyalties lay and we did not keep in touch after that. However, my sense of guilt over the toilet-paper incident at the club prompts me to call him back, though only with Anushka's sanction. I can't help it, I have a hyperactive conscience. Besides, Anushka is over him.

It is five past eight and here I am at Tabula Rasa, sitting across from the man whose face has adorned our dartboard for the last six months, his bulbous nose being the bull's-eye in our inebriated game of darts. He is not a good-looking man in the traditional sense, but he is well groomed. I know I make him sound like a horse, but believe me, he was into facials and manicures long before the advent of the metrosexual male. And to his credit, he always smells really nice—for a rat, that is.

"So how's the squash going?" I ask, trying to maneuver my thoughts in a different direction.

"It's okay. These past couple of months have

been rough, but I've thrown myself into work. And I also do yoga every morning and go swimming every day. Thirty laps," he says with pride.

"Uh-huh." One thing I can't connect with is physical exercise or exertion of any sort.

"Actually, today I did this colon-cleansing thing, where you drink water and then you keep going to the loo . . ."

This man has lost it. I am meeting him after months of distance and here he is talking about poop! Guess the toilet paper came in handy after all. He must have caught my vacant expression, for he stops. "Look at me going on about myself . . ."

"Not at all. We have a lot of catching up to do," I say, producing one of my well-rehearsed smiles.

"So how's Anu?"

"She's holding up fine, under the circumstances, you know." In reality, Anushka is doing better than just fine. She's not been this happy in years.

"You know about that night after the club? Anushka and I . . ."

"Yup." *Please don't go into the details.*

"It was magical . . ."

This is unnerving. Is the evening going to disintegrate into locker-room chat? We are definitely following the path—from poop to sex. Isn't that what boys usually discuss? Girlfriends, on the other hand, talk about men and sex. I already have way too much information about Anuj and his *little* friend. (Oops, didn't mean to give that away, but having your best friend's ex-husband share intimate details with you can have unexpected effects.)

"What did you want to talk about?"

"Do you think she'll take me back?"

"No." I state the fact, not knowing how else to say it.

"Sure?"

"Yes, and you should return the car. That was petty."

"My mom's idea." *But, of course, always the mother's idea.*

"Uh-huh, return it." Just when I am beginning to wonder whether the conversation is going to be reduced to monosyllabic questions and answers, Anuj changes track.

"Aisha, you're sort of about town and stuff. You know a lot of people. I'm going crazy here. Can you maybe introduce me around?"

"Are you asking me to fix you up?" I ask incredulously.

"No, I mean, I just need to meet new people."

"What happened to your friend? The reason we're having this conversation."

"It was an impulsive office thing and a huge mistake. I really do feel that Anu and I got married too early. Maybe if we had met now, things would have worked out. When we married, we were both so young. So, do you think you can help me out?" he presses on wistfully.

Why do men feel like victims even in situations that they are responsible for? They'll cheat on a woman and then come up with one of those clichéd excuses. It's almost as if all skirt-chasers have to go through the same orientation class before they are let loose in the dating world.

a) I was drunk, it happened by mistake
b) You don't make me feel man enough
c) It was just sex
d) We haven't been having great sex lately and I have my needs
e) All of the above

Gentlemen, what any intelligent, self-respecting woman would really want to hear is the truth. So try this version:

a) She was hot and available
b) I wanted to see if I still had it in me
c) I gave in to temptation
d) I never thought you'd find out
e) All of the above and especially option d

Let me make this simple. Infidelity = opportunity + availability.

But Anuj is looking so abject I don't know what to say. I glance at his hands resting on the table and do a double take. Is that a chipped nail? Oh, dear, this man is falling apart. The old Anuj would never have let it happen. It is a sure sign of mental distress, a cry for help. How can I just sit here and ignore it?

I tear my eyes away from his nails and say impulsively, "I'll do it."

I call Anushka once I get home, just to check if the best-friend part still holds.

"I committed to helping him."

"Aisha, you never commit, that's part of the problem."

"No, I did this time. He had chipped nails, so I agreed to help him jump-start his dating life."

"Please, like that makes sense! Never mind. How's he holding up? He was pretty psycho on some of the last phone calls."

"He was doing the psycho routine and you never warned me? Thanks! What if he'd drugged and gutted me and left me hanging from a telephone cord? Have you forgotten that *I* was the one caught with the toilet paper?"

"Aisha, honestly, your imagination! Why don't you just help him out? He needs to move on, really."

"Have you?"

"Yes, I have."

"You sure?"

"I'll tell you what, spend some time with him and then let's talk."

"It's just one evening out."

"Enjoy your date—and don't leave your drink unattended."

As in all times of moral peril or plain old bitchiness, I call the ex. My bitch fix is long overdue.

"Hi, you know Anuj and Anu split up and I've sort of promised to fix him up. I know you ho around town quite a bit, can you help him out?"

Okay, so he hangs up on me. I call back after the customary cooling-off period of about thirty seconds. And to think his chief grouse was that I never gave him any space! So I had broken up with him, but it's not like he had resisted it. In fact, many times I think that the split was all too easy, like he had sort of prompted it. I tried to get back with him after that, but he always responded with the convenient "too much water under the bridge" bullshit.

"I'm sorry, let me rephrase," I begin in a respectful tone. "As you are quite the man-about-town, I was hoping that maybe you could advise me on how to get my best friend's ex-husband a date."

"Are you listening to yourself, Aisha? You are pimping around for your best friend's husband!"

"Ex-husband, and I'm not 'pimping around,'" I say in a dignified tone. "Also, I have her blessing."

"Jeez, why do I even bother? You are all crazy. Try Arena on Thursday nights. It sounds right for your agenda. And, before you ask, no, I'm not getting involved."

So Anuj and I fix to go to Arena that Thursday night and Anushka is really impressed when, in a gesture of goodwill, the car is returned the very next day. In the days preceding our visit to Arena, I made it to the top list of Anuj's speed-dial, for he called me at least three or four times a day. If I didn't know him any better, I'd think he was suffering from some sort of bipolar disorder. He was optimistic and excitable during one conversation, and in the next he was stuck in the craters of despair. Having heard all that psychobabble from Anushka, I was always polite and took all his calls. Frankly, I was scared that he might do an SRK in that stalker flick. Although Indian matinee idol Shah Rukh Khan in a stalker movie is still sexy, while Anuj in stalker avatar is exactly what stalkers are meant to be: very scary.

That night at Athena, while Anuj and I sit at the bar, I focus my peepers on this new single guy on the block. Just then a pretty girl reaches between us to order her drink. She looks a bit like Anushka, so I turn to her, giving her my brightest smile. "Hi."

She looks back and smiles. "Hi, nice place."

"Yes, it is. It's crazy busy, the bartender will take his time getting to you."

"Looks like it."

"I'm Aisha and this is Anuj." Once the introductions are made, we sort of share the space for a bit in silence until I give Anuj the "get on with it" look.

As Anuj makes dull conversation, I listen in, feeling really sorry for him. I think men who get involved and subsequently marry really early miss out on the finer points of "scoping." Believe me, it's a jungle out there, and the hunting instinct needs to be constantly honed. Then Anuj does the smartest thing he's done all evening; he offers her his seat. I guess he isn't all that rusty after all.

"I'll go get you your drink. The bartender is not even looking in this direction."

"You don't have to, it's okay," the Anushka look-alike says. But he is already gone.

So it's just us gals. "He's a really sweet guy." I try putting in a good word for Anuj.

"Yes, he is, cute as well." Good, so not only does she have Anushka's looks, she also has her tastes. "Hope you don't mind me saying that." She giggles.

"No, not at all, women find him attractive all the time." I am overstating it, but what the hell.

"That doesn't bother you?" she asks curiously.

"Me? No, not at all. Why should it? The more the merrier, suits me fine. We don't have that kind of relationship."

"I see." She has a little frown on her face.

"Are you here alone?"

"I'm with some people from work. I don't really know anyone. I'm new here."

"Why don't you join us? I'd love it and I'm sure Anuj would as well. Let's make a night of it." I am going in all guns loaded.

Just then Anuj returns with the drink.

"Look, I think you guys are barking up the wrong tree. I've seen this stuff on TV, but I don't swing. Good luck." Having said that, she flees like a bat out of hell.

"What just happened here?" Anuj asks, confused.

He has as usual missed the punch line and is still clutching her shandy.

"Oh, don't worry about her," I say, "she has really tacky taste in alcohol."

Love Bites

Standing behind my desk at the Grand Orchid, I sometimes look at my colleagues and realize that we make quite a menagerie. There are the penguins—read butlers—whose coattails give flight to their rushed existence. Where's the fire, I intone irritably. I hate people running around in the lobby. It just conveys the wrong message to the guests, as though we don't quite have our act together. The key is "deliberate haste"—acting as if you are hurrying to fulfill your commitment to the guest, yet without displaying any undue anxiety or panic. I wish I could apply this axiom to my love life, but alas it never quite works that way. What I usually end up doing almost exclusively is rushing into everything and skinny-dipping in sleaze.

I look out beyond the doors of the lobby as I do on many a lazy afternoon, wishing to break free.

There stands Mahinder Singh, the doorman, in his harem pants, turban, and lofty mustache. He stands there twirling it distractedly and nodding in grim understanding as the mousy valet relates his latest antimanagement woes. What is with these people? I notice peevishly. Why work in a place that incites you to bitch all the time? And then I stop. Wait, why do I work here then?

Unanticipated insights are very disturbing, so I shift my gaze and rest it on Sneha, the new receptionist. Pretty as Barbie and as dumb as Ken. Wait, that's not nice. Ken wasn't really dumb, just dumb enough to be the perfect partner, and besides, he looked good. Hang on, I am digressing again, but Sneha really needs to up the intelligence quotient. I don't know how it's done at the ripe age of twenty-three, but it has to happen. Just yesterday she checked a guest into an occupied room and then batted her eyelashes and told me that the other guest didn't mind! *Didn't mind.* She meant that he didn't say a word to her. He spent a good forty-five minutes with me dissing everything from the hotel to the city to the government.

And then I notice Karan standing beside her with his bags, waiting to check out. I go over to say good-bye. In a purely professional capacity, of course.

"I was thinking of having a housewarming party. Nothing big, a few people from work and a few friends," Karan says as I approach them. He, of course, took the apartment that Tantalizing Tanya recommended.

"That's a great idea. When?" I dive straight into the conversation, giving Sneha the "Get about your work" officious look.

"Saturday night. I know it's short notice, but I'm just going to get busier from here on. Do you think you can help me? Look, if you're busy . . ." He mistakes my silence for a refusal.

"Sure, I'll help," I say quickly. I have to be careful. I don't want to sound overenthusiastic. I am busy, but what the hell. The image of Tantalizing Tanya in a hausfrau apron, passing around the hors d'oeuvres, is way too disconcerting. Damn it! It is going to be me in that apron!

Later that week I am at Karan's new apartment going over the list of invitees. Lenny Kravitz's *Ready for Love* is playing in the background. A sign, do you think? Okay, so the CD is on scramble and this is the eleventh track—not quite the stars lining up in my favor.

"What would you like to drink?"

"What do you have?"

"A lot. But how about we open a bottle of wine? There's this Chenin Blanc from Sula, looks interesting. Ever tried it?" He has discovered Sula on his own, I am so proud of him. Tried it? This stuff runs through my veins.

"Just a glass for me."

"Always playing it safe, Aisha." Karan winks.

You bet. I have worn my granny underwear tonight. Believe me, granny underwear is the chastity belt of our times. If one is ever in doubt of one's ability to control a potentially combustible situation, wear granny underwear. It's a very effective deterrent.

Karan has a stack of photographs on the coffee table. The most interesting one is of an older lady— very Gucci Mama—on her second face-lift for sure. She has those amazingly arched eyebrows that give the face a perpetual look of surprise. Maybe a brow lift: Misha would know. I make a mental list of all the possible cosmetic work done on Gucci Mama. This can be a fun party game. We can blow the picture up and have people guess at all the cosmetic work; the one with the largest number of correct answers will be the winner. Gosh, I am clever!

"That's Mom." And time stands still. Karan is behind me with the wine. Fortunately, he's missed the expression of utter guilt on my face.

"Oh, I thought she looked like you." Excellent comeback.

"Really? I'm told I look like my dad. My sister looks a lot like her. Sometimes people think they're sisters." He laughs. I am stuck, no clever comeback this time.

"She's coming down next month. You'll meet her then." Shoot, I begin to stress. I wonder how much Botox costs, or maybe some of that noninvasive surgery. Suddenly, I am painfully aware of the "indentations" on my forehead. You won't put a brown paper bag over my head yet, but age is creeping in.

Karan has a guest list of about twenty-five, but it's always safer to keep a margin of ten for any "friends of friends"—read gate-crashers—who come along. They inevitably waste no time making themselves more at home than the original invitees, but then, that's Delhi for you.

We decide on a barbecue. It involves a little bit of work, but it's going to be a beautiful late-November evening and Karan's apartment has a private terrace with a lovely view of a park, a rarity in this concrete jungle. We arrange for a local restaurant to do the catering. Nic knows of a bootlegger who is to deliver the alcohol—the imported, genuine stuff. We call him and add the mixers too to his list. Thus, in the tested tradition of the modern world, we do some effective outsourcing and sit in the moonlight sipping wine.

"It's fun organizing a party with you," Karan observes.

"Well, all we need is my little diary of numbers. My philosophy is, why do something when someone else can do it better?"

"Clever girl . . . I'm always afraid that the food will run out."

"Me too. I think I get that from my mom. Every time she threw a party, we ended up eating leftovers for the next five days." On second thought, it probably had little to do with quantity. I seem to remember seeing my dad slip some of the food to our dog. Flashbacks are so dangerous; they can change your whole view of life.

Karan smiles and gets up to refill my glass. We sit there for a long time in companionable silence and watch the evening stretch into night. On the one hand, I want to find out where we are headed, and on the other, I am perfectly content to sit here and share some quiet time with him. We are spending more and more time together. He is a good-looking man, and now I am on his balcony, ready and waiting. Yet he makes no moves. Granted, I am wearing granny underwear, but he has no means of knowing that. To the discerning eye, I am definitely presentable ("available" is too tacky a term). In fact, I might as well be holding a placard that says, "Kiss me, you fool."

I need some sort of reaction from this man. Maybe I can start the "I have to leave now" drama. It always works, and is a great way of figuring out what a guy has in mind. If he is interested in extending the evening, the "Stay a little longer" line will come into play. In this case, followed by "Let's move inside and listen to Lenny Kravitz and cuddle on the sofa, light a few candles . . ."

"It's getting late and the mosquitoes are chewing me up," Karan says, slapping his neck.

I am finally smacked out of my Mills and Boon–induced coma.

"Yes, it's getting late. I should be heading home."

"I guess so. It's going to be a long day tomorrow. Thanks so much for helping out." It looks like he knows exactly how this evening should turn out. Damn the mosquitoes, no, actually, damn him, why blame the poor little critters.

"No problem, anytime. I guess I'll see you tomorrow. Let me know if you need anything."

"Will do. Let me walk you to the car."

"Don't bother." I smile sweetly. "I'll be fine. You stay indoors, the mosquitoes may attack again. Besides there is this particular aggressive strain of malaria doing the rounds." I shut the door in his face, with a somewhat concerned smile.

His lingering look of muted horror is enough to confirm one fact for me: Visitors to our country are almost always concerned about contracting something. And sometimes I am not above doing a bit of auto-suggesting on my own. Besides I had just answered one of the more pressing queries of the evening. I knew exactly what he was getting for a housewarming present now. You got it! Mosquito repellent.

The moment I get home I dial my midnight bitching partner. (Misha is my early-morning bitching partner.)

"Anushka," I fume over the phone. She is dead asleep, but I have to let off steam.

"What's happened? Everything okay?" she mumbles.

"Everything's fine, just great. I don't know what he thinks I am!"

"I take it the evening with Karan did not go as planned." She yawns.

"Stop yawning. I don't know what I've become. It's like I'm party planner, chief adviser, court jester, and girl Friday all rolled into one."

"Come on! No one can be that perfect!" Anushka laughs.

"No, really, this is serious. I sat there doing my best Angelina Jolie pout, and this guy is the p-i-t-t-s."

"Look, the first kiss is the best, most spectacular, cloud-burst moment in a relationship. It can't happen on cue. If it does, it's so trite, you know, *boring*. It has to happen when you least expect it," Anushka explains wisely.

"Yeah, like the time the ex and I were making out and Mama Bhatia decided to leave a long message on the answering machine about my *alleged* weight gain."

"It wasn't 'alleged.' " Anushka giggles.

"Your interest in trivial details is very annoying. Good night, Anushka."

"Good night, princess. Just remember it's all in the kiss. So if you're not ready to find out, just carry on waltzing."

Does Anushka have a point? When will this dizzying waltz end? Maybe I am stepping on his toes? Or is he the one missing all the cues?

No Garlic, No Onion

What are your views on pyaaz and garlic?"

"They are vegetables, Ma. I mean, what time is it?"

"It's seven-thirty. Why are you not up as yet? Aren't you doing that ritual with the Shivling?" My mother is sounding breathless and excited.

For the uninitiated, the ritual with the Shivling assures you a good mate. All you have to do is place it in the sun and pour water over it at sunrise. There is no proof that it actually works. I even checked with Misha, my dial-a-marital-anecdote friend, but she could not come up with anything. And, frankly, I am just so not into worshipping phallic symbols.

"Listen to me, there is this boy—" My mom has a great stress defense mechanism. The moment she realizes that a query posed by her has been replied to in the negative, she pretends like she never posed it in the first place. "—he works for McKinsey in New York, has done his MBA. Only problem, he is a pucca vegetarian, no garlic and onions even. I think after all the diets you've been on, this should be no problem," she says with confidence.

This is true. I spent a good part of the last decade dieting. They truly were my salad years, until I discovered the Atkins diet. But if it is the care that vegetables and herbs are a relevant basis for marriage, then here is my requirement based on the food-group philosophy: I want a guy who does only high protein and no carbs. I'll even settle for a low-carb guy, but only if he is completely worth it. I mean no disrespect for anyone's beliefs, but I do think it is time I have my own set of demands. Besides, who wants to belo rotis, so totally regressive to roll out those little Indian tortillas, when you can even get daal in a can.

"No problem, Ma, just make sure he is on high proteins and no carbs."

"What?"

"Okay, we can go South Beach. He can eat salads."

"Aisha, you are making no sense. I hope you are not doing those drugs, which is the one named after the cold drink?"

I hang up. How dare my mom think my life is so debauched! I don't do drugs and I left early-morning drinking behind in the nineties—talk about regressive! This has to be kalyug, the time of evil and moral decline in Hindu mythology, with mothers including drugs in their vocabulary. I tell you, parents these days! I slump back into dreamless slumber.

I wake up remembering that I hung up on my mom. Shoot! It will take a whole day to placate her.

"Ma, I'm sorry about this morning. The phone got disconnected."

"It's fine, beta, I am used to it." The worst is when my mother plays the injured party.

"No, really, it did get disconnected."

"Anyway, the proposal is off."

"Oh?"

"If you cannot show respect for their traditions, then you don't deserve to belong to their family." I am dumbstruck. The ability to truly appreciate the nuances of our ancient culture has always eluded me. In my desire to be a liberated Indian woman, am I missing out on the basics? Are garlic and pyaaz integral to my existence? "Besides, he's twenty-six years old," my mother concludes. Great! So that's the real reason. I have been eliminated for the most innocuous reason: age.

The conversation with my mother gets me thinking. Is my age beginning to show? If so, I must do something about it. I head straight for the torture chamber.

"Welcome, welcome, you should have told me you were coming. I would have arranged for the band." It is Boom Voice Raghav, my gym instructor, heralding my return after two months. "Let's start with getting you onto the weighing scale." *Like the loud welcome is not humiliation enough.* "Not bad, just five kilos, unlike the last time you disappeared. . . . It was seven, remember?" he says gleefully. Raghav has this big voice in a bigger body, and it can carry for kilometers, believe me.

"Hi, Aisha, you're a member of this gym too?" Karan asks with a smile. Shit! For a moment, all I can do is worry about whether he has heard Raghav's moving announcement.

"In the loosest sense of the word," I say, jumping off the weighing machine, which gratefully squeaks back to zero.

"You know each other?" Boom Voice butts in. "Maybe you can learn some discipline from Karan. He is so fit, great body." *You're telling me.*

"Anyway, let me get you on the treadmill. If you have a flat tire, the one around your belly will help . . . Let's go." He guffaws at his own poor joke. I could die right at that moment. But I shrug nonchalantly and follow Boom Voice obediently.

What is it with trainers? How do they figure they can say anything to you at any time? It's true, of course, that your personal trainer is the only guy in the world that you can talk to about your boobs, I mean really talk. You know, stuff like how big they are, the way they sag, how to firm them up, etc. It's a strangely intimate relationship, necessitated by pure and cold-blooded clinical vanity. Women never acknowledge this relationship, but it exists. It is my belief that in some disco-music-blaring corner of every gym, wherever in the world it is, you'll find a damsel in calorific distress revealing her woes to the one person who is paid to listen. Let's be honest here: How many times have you seen a perky twenty-something jogging on a treadmill and tried to figure out if she is wearing a support bra? Women past a certain age pay almost as much attention to boobs as pubescent boys. Anyway, to get all Freudian, I am clearly feeling overweight at this point. I wish I had worn my sports bra. And I wonder just how many perky twenty-somethings have their eyes on well-toned Karan.

"Aisha, what time are you coming tonight?" Karan is standing next to me as I huff and puff at an embarrassing speed of 4.5 on the treadmill.

"I thought around eight, or do you need help? I can come over earlier," I offer cheerfully, increasing the speed to a more respectable 5.5.

"No, please, you've been a great help already. I hope your friends are coming?"

"Misha and Anushka are, the others have plans." I am up to 6 and jogging. I know most people walk at that speed. I am not most people.

"That's great. Do you need to be picked up? I can have my driver come get you guys."

"No...uh...we'll make it." I gasp. I am running at 7.

"Aisha, are you okay? You're going all red in the face."

"I'm...fine." Damn, I can't get my finger on the speed button. Why does he just keep standing there?

"Stop pehalwan...Are you trying to kill yourself?" Boom Voice Raghav dramatically pushes the emergency switch. I manage a watery smile as the treadmill comes to an abrupt halt.

"I guess I will see you tonight," Karan says with a measure of uncertainty in his voice. It's really more of a question than a statement. I respond with a smile and a nod, too breathless to answer.

As he walks away, Boom Voice Raghav takes over. "If you overdo it today, you won't return for the next six months. And when you do, God knows how much weight you will have gained."

That evening Misha and Anushka reach my home to find me flat on my back. "Why aren't you ready yet?" Misha exclaims.

"I have a stiff neck."

"Oh, dear, what happened?" Anushka asks.

"Do you know that some women wear makeup to the gym?"

"You mean you don't?" Misha gives me an incredulous look.

"Aisha, what happened?" Anushka repeats patiently.

"That's why they created waterproof mascara," Misha continues, shaking her head in disapproval.

"I went to the gym today and Karan was there and Raghav was being obnoxious, so I did too many sit-ups and shoulder presses and stressed my neck out."

"But this has happened before! Why aren't you more careful?" Anushka is not going to let me off lightly.

"So, was Karan in shorts? Does he look hot? Does he do that whole ganji thingy?" Misha's totally missing the point. Anushka silences her with a glare.

"I really want to go, but I don't know how. I can't even pick out my clothes," I moan.

"Sweetie, don't worry about that, you just lie there." Anushka will be a great mom someday. That's if she ever gets into the whole domesticity thing again.

"And I'll do your makeup while you lie down, and sprinkle perfume on your hair and behind your ears," Misha joins in. She would have made a great concubine in the old world.

"Wear the black polo neck and jeans. It won't draw too much attention to your neck. Very chic."

"I don't care if it's chic or a shriek. I just need to get ready and get to that party."

"Of course you do. Don't be silly. We'll have you fixed in no time."

The Housewarming

*A*s if my day isn't bad enough, the limp-wristed Tanya opens the door to Karan's apartment. "Welcome, come on in!" *Great, she is playing hostess!*

"Isn't that the latest Shantanu and Nikhil, the must-have look for the season?" Misha whispers as we follow Tantalizing Tanya into Karan's home.

I ignore her remark. I feel so cheated. Betrayed by Gudda for dressing my rival and by Misha for acknowledging it. Betrayed by Karan for letting Tanya play hostess when I have spent the last couple of hours trying to knock my body into some kind of shape just for him and this stupid party.

As Misha and Anushka go off to get me a drink, I sit down on the couch, as erect as a beanpole. Right in my line of vision is the silver-framed photograph of Gucci Mama. She occupies pride of place on the coffee table. Karan is definitely a mama's boy.

"So you made it." Karan sinks onto the couch next to me. "I saw you come in and tried to catch your eye, but you weren't looking."

"I'm sorry I missed you," I say, still looking straight ahead.

"That's my mother, the same photograph you saw the other day."

Gosh, he must think I am a freak, eyeballing his mother like that! "I know, I was just admiring the frame." I turn my entire body to face him and it's suddenly a very uncomfortably intimate situation. Here we are on a two-seater among at least thirty people. This is not how I had planned our Mills and Boon moment. Karan gives me this intense look and says nothing. I search frantically for something intelligent to say.

"Here's your wine." Misha encroaches with the enthusiasm of a fire extinguisher and defuses the sparks.

"Thank you," I say, taking my glass and averting my gaze.

Karan gets up and offers his place. "Glad you could make it."

"Thanks for inviting us, great apartment."

"Thank you, I still need to get a lot done."

"The only thing missing is a woman's touch," Misha says slyly.

"Well, my mom is coming in about a month. So I think that's going to be taken care of." Misha rolls her eyes and I whisper to her to shut up.

"Karan," Tanya chirps, "I can't find the wine opener, can you help me?" *Just use your fangs, missy.*

"Sure. Ladies, if you will excuse me."

As I try to appear lost in my drink, I chance upon a familiar face. It is the Anushka look-alike from the other night. She catches my eye at the same time and I raise my hand in a wave, but her disgusted expression catches me midway. Right, humiliated once more. No problem, I'm getting used to this. Maybe I can play snake on my phone. Now, where is my bag? Great, it's resting at my feet. I will have to bend down at a perfect ninety-degree angle to lift up the bag. This promises to be more fun than playing snakes. I am wearing high-heeled boots. Therefore, I have two options: slide the handle across my heel and lift the bag, or balance the bag between my feet and lift it up discreetly. Option two is much quicker, so it wins out.

As I jostle with the bag between my boots, I feel a tap on my shoulder. I think it's sheer shock that makes me turn my neck. I hear it snap. "Ouch," I yelp.

"Aisha, are you okay?" It's Karan, looking worried. That's the second time he's asked me the question in twenty-four hours. Which can't be a good thing.

"I'm all right. I have a stiff neck from the workout," I say, rubbing the painful area. Through the curtain of a tearful haze, like a blinking mirage, the Anushka look-alike takes form. Except that it's not a mirage, it's the real deal. What is she doing with Karan? And she looks far from happy.

"I want you to meet my cousin Natasha, my maasi's daughter. She's just moved here too."

Natasha looks at me with utter distaste. I hope silently that Karan has missed it.

"I was telling Natasha what a great friend you've been helping me settle in. I was hoping that you'd guide my little coz as well."

"Sure, I'm all yours," I say glibly, trying to cover up the awkwardness.

She gives me another disgusted look.

"I'll leave you two girls alone then. I can see my boss looking around. Thanks, Aisha." Karan gives me the cutest wink. I watch his retreating butt until Natasha speaks up.

"Does bhaiyya know about your *other* interests?" she says archly, raising one eyebrow. How do people manage to raise one eyebrow like that? It has always fascinated me, the amazing facial motor control it must require. I have never been able to do it.

"Look, Natasha, you've got it all wrong, I was not trying to pick you up. Well, actually, I was trying to pick you up, not for me, or for us, but just for my friend."

Natasha keeps staring at me. "Okay, not really a friend. He used to be one. You see that girl there," I say, pointing to Anushka, "she's my best friend and he was married to her."

"And now you are dating him?" Natasha raises the other eyebrow. Just how does she do it? If we ever get through this conversation, I will ask her to teach me.

"No, I was helping him find a date. I felt bad for him and she said it was okay."

"Bhaiyya thinks you're cute, but honestly, you are one strange chick," Natasha says, getting up.

"Bhaiyya, I mean Karan, thinks I'm cute?" I splutter.

"I have to go, okay? I don't know what to say to people like you. Good luck, I guess."

Frankly, I am past caring what Ms. I-never-get-my-panties-in-a-wire has to say. Bhaiyya thinks I am cute and that is awesome. I am glad I came after all.

"Why are you grinning like a Cheshire cat?" Anushka is back from her social stint.

"Bhaiyya thinks I'm cute."

"I'm sorry? Did you take painkillers before the wine?"

"No, silly. Karan thinks I'm cute."

"And you know this how?"

"Well, his cousin told me. Remember I told you about that girl at Arena? She's his cousin."

"That's not a good thing."

"Plain misunderstanding, we sorted it out."

"You sure?"

"Who cares! Anyway, he thinks I'm cute."

"Hmm, I met an old colleague from work and we are looking at future business opportunities. I think this could work."

"Is he married?"

"Aisha, you're talking like Misha. Relax, will you? His marital status has nothing to do with the amount of money he can help me make."

"Why are you getting upset?"

"Because that's really all the two of you can talk about these days. Why didn't he call, why didn't he kiss me, what car does he drive, where does he work . . . There's more to life than men." I look at Anushka, taken aback by her sudden outburst. "Look, you guys stay on, I have to head home."

"We'll all leave."

"No, you stay. Misha is out there flirting with some guy. I'm not in the mood. I just need to be alone." She picks up her clutch and stalks off.

I don't get it. Just what did I say? Sometimes women can't understand each other either. It's not just men who have that problem.

I get off the couch and go in search of Misha. I find her leaning against a pillar and listening in rapt attention to a guy who, in all likelihood, is a stock-broker. I perform the "do you need rescuing" gal-pal maneuver, which comprises of standing behind the guy and raising an eyebrow—both, in my case. I wish I could do the one-eyebrow lift. Anyhow, here is how it works: If she needs help, she'll draw me into the conversation and we'll make an excuse and run. If it's going well, she'll just ignore me and I'll leave.

Misha ignores me and gushes loudly, "You work in the wealth management division? How interesting." I know how Misha's mind works. The only interesting part is the wealth bit. She probably figures that if he manages wealth, he must have some of his own. I shake my head and continue on my way.

So here I am, almost single at this party. My best

friend has just walked out, the host is too busy for me, his cousin thinks I'm a freak, and Tantalizing Tanya has usurped my role as hostess par excellence. The good news is that the wine and the painkiller I took earlier are starting to take effect. Although I'm alone, and know almost no one, and am liked by only half of those who know me, the party is beginning to rock. I reach for another glass of Sula and drink it in quick gulps. Chilled Chenin Blanc equals major head rush. *Yippee.*

I decide to cool off on the terrace and take another faithful glass with me. I pull out a cigarette and look for a flame when it magically appears in front of me.

"Thanks." I giggle.

"No problem." He smiles back.

"Who are you?"

"Sharad. And you?"

"Aisha."

"You are very beautiful, Aisha."

"Thank you."

"Are you here with someone?"

"No, all alone. Really alone."

"You don't need to be."

"Really? How do you know that?"

"Because I can see something that you don't."

"Ooooh, and what do you see, Mr. Suresh?"

"Sharad."

"Yeah, whatever."

"I see someone very beautiful who doesn't need to be alone."

"Hmmph."

"That's all I get? 'Hmmph'? How about we leave here," he says, putting his hands on my shoulders.

"Ouch!" I feel a spasm in my neck.

"Are you okay?"

"I have a stiff neck."

"I can fix it." He stands in front of me and places both palms on my cheeks. I can feel his hot fetid breath on my nose.

"Aisha." A voice from the doorway breaks into what appears to be an awkwardly intimate scene. It's Karan and he looks furious. Or am I imagining it? "There's a call for you," he says, a semblance of calm returning to his voice, "in the room at the back."

I wriggle out of Suresh's—sorry, Sharad's—grasp and walk past Karan. Sharad turns around regretfully and leans over the balcony.

I manage to find the room. It is a bedroom with one of those minimalist futon-style beds and a phone on a low table. I slump on the bed and pick up the receiver. There is no one at the other end. Maybe Anushka has hung up. I try to call her but can't remember the number. Is it 9819 or 9891? Perhaps I'll just sit here and wait for her to call back.

I awake to the sound of humming and the steady trickle of water. My head feels like a ton of bricks, and it's with great effort that I lift it from the pillow. As I wipe the drool from the corner of my mouth, I hear him. "So you're up?" Karan is looking unbelievably sexy in a towel and wet hair. He has one of those amazingly smooth, hairless chests. *He must have to wax for that look!*

"I don't know why I'm here."

"Well, I do. You took over my bedroom last night."

"How did I get here?"

"Temptation led you here . . . Can I put on some clothes and then we can continue with the inquisition?"

"Oops, I'm sorry," I say, lowering my gaze.

"I like it when you blush."

"What?" I call out to his retreating figure.

"Nothing. I said you can go back to sleep, no rush."

Ah, so he's playing my word game. I turn to look at the other side of the bed; it has not been slept in. I guess he slept in the guest room.

I get out of bed and find a mirror. Shoot, my bed-head look is not at all appealing. My morning breath is 180-proof alcohol, and there is mascara streaming down my face. I am the poster child for what you don't want your daughters to be when they grow up: prostrate in a strange man's bed, with no recollection of what happened the previous night. I find my brush, run it through my matted hair, and frantically wash my face. It makes little difference visually, but psychologically I feel rejuvenated. I pull out my little airline toothbrush and manage to scrub some of the nicotine stains from my teeth. Then, courageously, I wind my way to his kitchen.

As I pour myself a tall glass of water, I meditate on how I have succeeded in making an utter fool of myself. And then my eyes fall on a stack of papers. Right on top is a printout of an email. I'm not sneaky by nature, but this is sitting right there. I crane my neck in an attempt to read it. Can you blame me? Strange, when motivated enough, the neck works just fine despite the stiffness. It's called mind over body, baby. The email is in a bold font and the subject column says: "Marital Alliance." And then it proceeds with a description. I pick it up and read it with a sense of mounting panic. The marriage proposal spells out the details of some girl who lives in Mumbai. She is twenty-four years old, convent educated—I thought that was rather passé—and has gotten her MBA from one of those foreign universities that you can study at while living in India. She is tall, slim, and fair with sharp features. *Aren't they all?* She claims to be a good classical dancer and has done some fancy cookery course in Italy. Basically, she has gone to the school of the "future brides of desis abroad." The missive instructs Karan to give her a call at some point during the week. This is really quite progressive. Perhaps Gucci Mama is loosening the reins.

I suddenly feel a knot in my stomach. Karan is bride hunting! Maybe his family is doing the looking. No, I'm not going to make any excuses for the man. I've heard that many NRIs love the idea of a born-and-bred Indian girl for a bahu, a daughter-in-law. Supposedly, we Indian gals are susheel or something—we have good values. Little do they know that New Delhi is in some ways far ahead of New Jersey. I think they assume that the study of "good traditional values" is an elective course offered to women in our schools because it is mentioned unfailingly whenever there is talk of an "alliance."

I don't stand a chance. Like Misha, I can't even tell my daals apart, and the only way I'll listen to bhajans is if they start remixing them and playing them on MTV.

"Still wondering how you got here?" Karan returns in his track pants and tee, looking freshly scrubbed and clean. I hastily push the paper into my pocket.

"Yup," I say, running a distracted hand through my hair and realizing what a close shave it has been. He probably won't miss it.

"You were a little tipsy and insisted on spending the night." Karan grins.

"Look, I'm not a lush. I know your intentions are good. But you're a product of an 'overpsychologized' society, namely the U.S. of A., where everyone has an issue. Get this—I don't have an issue with alcohol. I have an issue with a low alcohol tolerance level."

Karan looks a little taken aback at my unprovoked outrage and then bursts out laughing. He laughs for a good five minutes. What's wrong with him? I think what I said was perfect. "I'm sorry," he says, sobering up. "It was just a joke. What I want to really say is that you fascinate me and amuse me, and I love being around you."

"Sure." I try to sound casual. *Then why are you looking for a decent convent-educated type?*

Karan leans forward and looks into my eyes. "I think it was the moment I saw you in those Jackie O shades. . . ." And then he kisses me. Just like that.

As kisses go, it's quite pedestrian. But confusing. I need to get away. As I stand there reeling from the impact of his kiss, Karan strokes my hair and asks me what I want to have for lunch.

"Lunch? What time is it? I have to be at work at two. I need to get home."

"You have to eat."

"No, I have to work to keep my job, so I can eat. I should leave."

And so, without even waiting for a response, I make my disgraceful flight—I don't even bother to wear my shoes or wait for the elevator, and run down the stairs two at a time. I need to call Misha to piece the evening back together, to truly understand what happened.

Boss's Wife Management

"The Grand Orchid, good afternoon."

"Hello, the lobby, please."

"Reception, how may I help you?" Shit, it's Rajat, my pompous-ass colleague and the boss's chief chamcha, or hanger-on.

"Hi, Rajat, this is Aisha. I'm running about fifteen minutes late. Terrible traffic."

"Ooh, not good, the boss is very upset today."

"Is he PMS-ing again?" I know as I speak that it's going to be repeated verbatim to the boss. But I have to "fake bond" with this jerk for I'm going to be late by half an hour, not fifteen minutes.

"Ha, ha, Aisha, you are so funny! Don't worry, okay, drive safe."

My boss and Rajat are the Batman and Robin of our office. I can't decide which one I dislike more. It's a toss-up on any given day. At least Rajat does some work. He is a pompous ass, but at least he has an ass that moves. He is one of those who doesn't get his coat dry-cleaned at the uniform room because it is not good enough and instead spends five hundred bucks for express service once every three days at a posh city dry cleaner. He also has an ample number of women chasing his coattails, especially the new graduates in their first jobs.

Rajat is a little wary of me because I once caught him at a nightclub with one of those "chicks with dicks," so hard to identify in today's gender-bending world. Ric knew her/him from somewhere, and when we saw Rajat in a corner, getting all heavy and hot, we went and greeted them, Ric using "her" real name, which turned out to be Parwinder. She nearly bitch-slapped Ric, while poor Rajat looked trauma-tized and ran. We never, ever spoke about it, but he knows that I know and that's good enough. And I'm not above taking the occasional cheap shot at him in front of his potential conquests. Stuff like "What's your favorite movie, Rajat? *Tootsie* or *The Adventures of Priscilla, Queen of the Desert,* maybe even *Chachi No. 1*?"

I make it to the locker room and realize I have done it again—I have forgotten my petticoat at home. Damn! I'll have to tie my sari over my jeans. I've done it so many times now that I am an expert, but it's uncomfortable. Worse, it always makes me look fatter. People always wonder why I have not met a nice young man at work yet. It's because of the sari—I call it the male repellent. Yes, I know a lot of women look stunning in it. I am not one of those women. On a good day, I look like a well-draped potato. And there are enough bad days when I end up wearing it over my jeans. It's a basic design flaw: Saris should come with a stitched-on petticoat. I must convey this suggestion to Gudda.

I walk out of the locker room twenty-two minutes later and spot my boss closeted in his office. I stick my head into the operator's cabin and ask, "Is he on the phone?"

The ever-efficient and inquisitive head operator looks at her board. "For the last twenty-five minutes. It's his wife, I think, she's yelling at him."

She's been eavesdropping again.

"Thanks." My boss's love life is of utmost interest to the entire hotel staff. There is a wife and a girlfriend, and we love to observe him juggle the two.

"I recognized the voice when I connected him," she explains sullenly, reading my mind. "It's the wife, not the girlfriend."

"Thanks again."

"One day he'll get caught. Really, one day I'll cause a cross-connection when he is talking to his girlfriend. The way he came in and shouted at me today . . ." she grumbles. I shut the door in the middle of her diatribe. Luckily, the cabin is soundproof. They don't call them the "bitches on switches" for nothing.

———

It feels as if the boss has two wives. Even his girl-friend behaves like the wife. She must be the worst-kept secret in our department. The only thing going in her favor is that she has old D.P.G. on his toes. If he ever misses her call, it's like a game of twenty questions: "When did she call," "Did you tell her where I was," etc., etc. One time I had the distinct pleasure of holding wife and girlfriend on separate lines simultaneously, both insisting on speaking to the boss. Unfortunately, he was with the GM, so it didn't quite work out. God must be a man. How else does one account for the burgeoning number of phi-landerers who never get caught!

It's also thanks to the girlfriend that our boss works on Sundays. Rumor has it that she does not want him spending the day with his wife, so he takes his weekly day off on Tuesdays. We, therefore, have the pleasure of his company on Sundays, the one chilled-out day of the week when we could have played hooky.

"The boss has been asking for you for the last fif-teen minutes. I had to keep making excuses." Rajat makes it very clear that he has been covering for me. Sure, he must have been asking for me between getting yelled at by his wife—"Honey, can you stop yelling for a second, I need to check if Aisha has come in."

"Really? Thanks so much." I smile insincerely.

"Aisha, Rajat, can you come into my office?" It's the boss. What is this about and why am I being in-cluded in the discussion? Finally part of the boys' club and I don't even have my acceptance speech ready!

"Hurry up, Aisha!" his little lapdog says, running ahead.

We enter the boss's love chamber. "Guys, I cannot be disturbed. You will need to handle the lobby on your own today." So what is new about that? "I have work to do." Now that is something new. "Too much pending stuff, so I need you all to manage on your own."

"No problem, boss, we've got it covered," Rajat says, stepping up to the plate. Why is it that I'm always tongue-tied when it comes to making these grandiose statements?

"Yes, sir, it's just the brunch crowd. Nothing will happen today," I say, not wishing to be left out yet again.

"Aisha, no casual attitude today. Don't leave the lobby for a moment, no smoke break, no lipstick break. Okay?" *Should I kick him in the balls now or later?* "Rajat, I need to show you some papers." That's my cue, so I turn and leave. I will plot his downfall with the head operator later. He definitely has it coming.

I barely reach my desk in the lobby when in walks the girlfriend. I flash one of my big ones, gums and all.

"Hi, Aisha. You're looking lovely. I just love the way you drape your sari. You must tell me your secret." The other woman is always really nice—it's like she is in this constant Ms. Congeniality battle with the real Mrs.

"I wear it over jeans." I grin.

"Naughty girl. Don't worry, I won't tell him."

Like the boss really wants to know what lies under my sari. It's Rajat who needs to develop an insight into these matters.

Just then the lapdog appears. "Oh, Ms. Ruby, you're looking wonderful today. Let me take you to the office." *What's with this guy? Does he have a book on lick-ass quotes?*

"Ciao."

"Bye, Ms. Ruby."

The girlfriend isn't such a bad sort. She is actually very good-looking in a high-maintenance sort of way. She could have almost any man she wants. Why then is she stuck on my potbellied married boss? Sadly, there are women like that who have an exclusive preference for men who are already taken. It's the challenge, the unattainability factor that gets them going. But the belly . . . I can't explain that.

Just then the door opens and in walks the real Mrs. She strides into the lobby along with an older lady.

"Good afternoon, ma'am."

"Good afternoon, Aisha. How are you?"

"Very well, thank you."

"Can you page my husband and let him know I'm here?" she orders. "Ma, why don't you sit down," she says, turning to the older lady. Perfect. My faith in God is all restored. Wifey and ma-in-law have come visiting.

I try the boss's extension and find it busy. The wife is standing near at hand, impatiently tapping a scarlet nail on the counter. I call the head operator.

"Neerja, can you dial Sir's extension and tell him Ma'am is here in the lobby?"

"Isn't one Mrs. already locked up in his office with him?" Neerja giggles.

"Right. Neerja, will you please try? I'll hold." I try to sound very professional.

"Has it been busy lately?" The wife tries to make conversation.

"Not at all. Occupancy has been down."

"Really? Tutu has been working late every night," she says suspiciously.

"Oh, Sir has a lot of other responsibilities, reports and all." I try to sound convincing. I solemnly apologize to the global sisterhood, but I have to eat.

"Why haven't they called back?" she snaps after a while.

"I'll try again, ma'am." I pick up the phone. "Neerja, did you get through?"

"No, Aisha. Do you want me to interrupt? It's probably an official call since all his women are here. Unless, of course, he's taken the phone off the receiver so he's not disturbed. . . ."

The Mrs. is leaning in to listen. Shoot! I have to think fast. I am sure Rajat is on his smoke break. "Thanks, Neerja, keep trying, please," I say and quickly hang up, before she incriminates us all.

"So, still busy?"

"I'm afraid so."

"That's okay, this will just take a minute. I'll go around to his office."

"He's not there."

"But you were trying his office right now and the number was busy."

Gosh, she is sharp!

"I have to drop something off." She strides off before I can stop her. I run after her as there is nothing better to say or do. Honestly, I am deriving immense pleasure from this whole situation. *Forgive me, God, if you're a man, and Hallelujah if you're a woman.*

As the Mrs. races ahead of me in her heels, I make a feeble attempt to stop her, just in case someone is watching. "Ma'am, I can take the package and give it to him." She ignores me and keeps moving. The door is shut. "Looks like he's not here, ma'am."

"No, the light is on," she says and tries the doorknob. Wow, this woman is good. How has he gotten away with it for so long?

"It's locked. He never locks the door. He must be someplace else." The Mrs. by this point is not even listening to me. She starts to knock on the door and then tragically breaks a beautifully manicured nail.

"Shit, I'll have to go to the nail bar," she says with frustration rising in her voice.

"I'll do it, ma'am." It is purely her anxiety level that makes me offer to bang on the door. Okay, maybe it's also a little curiosity and plain old bitchiness. If Tutu is getting his horn tooted, he has to be found out!

I pound on the door, but there is no response. Perhaps the boss isn't in, after all. I actually feel a

sense of relief. The truth be told, I hate confrontation in any form. I mean, we all love the prospect of a
potential conflict, especially one that's illicit or spicy,
but more in the capacity of a spectator, not as an active participant.

I have to admit that I sort of get carried away with
the banging. It is the total vibe of the situation. As I
initiate another bout of furious pounding, I turn to
look at the Mrs. for affirmation and appreciation. I
nearly fall on my face when the door suddenly
swings open. My boss stands there with his gelled
hair looking a little mussed up. Behind him on the
sofa sits Ms. Ruby with her legs tucked under her
cute little behind. No way will the candidate-for-
interview excuse work for her.

As my generous frame hides the petite Mrs., the
boss growls, "What's the matter, Aisha, where's the
fire?" *Hopefully up your ass.*

"Hi, baby!" Ms. Ruby exclaims from the couch.
The Mrs. emerges from my shadow and saves me
the agony of a suitable response.

"Hi, Ruby, what are you bothering your jiju
for?" Have I just got this right? *Jiju?* That must make
them . . . wait . . . that's right . . . The Mrs. and the
girlfriend are sisters!

"Tutu, Mama is waiting outside. Here's the envelope. Anyway, I have to run now. Are you coming
home early today?"

"Depends . . ." the boss says.

"I'll also come along," Ms. Ruby says, getting up.

"No, it's okay," says the Mrs. "I have to take Mama

to the doctor. I'm sure this is more fun." She walks off.

"Aisha, I told you not to leave the lobby." The boss looks at me sorely.

"I'm sorry, sir," I mumble. Why am I embarrassed?

I get back to my desk in a state of bewilderment and with the realization that my ass is grass. As I sit down, the phone rings.

"So, did he get caught?" Neerja is gloating.

"No, he did not. Get back to work," I say and hang up on her. I am in management. They need to treat me with a little deference.

I sit there and ponder what has just transpired. I have heard of the blended family, but this is a different ball game. It lends a whole new meaning to keeping it all in the family. Of course, we Indians grow up on stories of multiple bonding. I remember I was in the sixth grade when we studied the *Mahabharata*, and Draupadi didn't scandalize me even then. This was, of course, before we learned of the mysteries of sex. In any case, that was mythology and this is reality. However, I can't reconcile with this reality. Strange as it is, I don't need a man to pay my bills, but I do need him to give me his last name.

Born-Again Virgin

*L*ata Didi calls the next morning. She is back from her trip home to Nashik and wants me to come over and collect the comfort package my mother has sent me. Believe me, the term "comfort package" is highly misleading. Sometimes I feel if I were married, Mama Bhatia would actually make an attempt to send me something useful, if only to impress the ma-in-law or the spouse. I know I am playing the ungrateful child but someone please give me a use for a mortar and pestle. I promise to go across after work to collect it. It is one of those chores that I would gladly put off for a couple of days, except it will send the totally wrong impression to the maika, the parental home, and Nina Maasi in particular. I would subsequently find myself at the receiving end of grave disapproval.

Later that evening I find myself standing on a

coir mat that says Welcome. Lata Didi answers the door on the second ring and crushes me to her ample bosom.

"Coir mats are tacky."

"Really, save the advice for when you have your own home," my cousin retorts.

"Meow. What's wrong with you? Was a month in the parental home too long?"

"That reminds me, when are you going home? Maasi misses you like crazy."

I close the door behind me but don't answer. It is very important not to commit to anything in front of Lata Didi, even vacation dates. Before you know it, it will be communicated on the hotline back home. And then my mother will start hyperventilating about how I never share anything with her.

"So where's Jiju?"

"Traveling as usual." Did I detect a note of resentment? Nah, can't be, they have a model marriage. "What will you have to drink?"

"Nothing. So where's the package?"

"Look at you, excited like a child!"

"You know me . . ."

She brings out one of those mango crates. Maybe she has sent me mangoes. That would be great, but it isn't the season and I am never that lucky. I tear open the box. It contains the usual stuff: a bottle of pickled vegetables that I will never eat; some buknu, an eastern U.P. digestive eaten during meals that I don't need since I've given up eating; a floral bedspread that I will never use, or maybe can sometimes use as a curtain to completely block out the sun. And then there is the pièce de résistance, a photograph of some sort of a sadhu that is so large that it will need its own little attic to be hidden in.

Mama Bhatia calls at that very moment. "Beta, did you get the parcel?"

"Yes, thank you, who's the dude?"

"What?"

"The baba."

"Oh, that's Swami Raman. He's very powerful. Remember Goel Aunty's daughter, Minku? She was having trouble finding a match. So they started going to Swami Raman and in two months she was engaged."

"Really? Minku's engaged?" I remember Minku as a sullen horse-faced teenager. I also recall all the neighborhood aunties clucking sympathetically over her. She was said to have "such a long face and a *daba hua* complexion," which basically is the politically correct term for dark-skinned. It was prophesied that she would be the last to get married. Guess I am the one who turned out to be the black sheep.

"Yes, beta, everyone is . . ." My mother's voice holds a note of sorrow.

"So this baba is very powerful?" I change the subject with faux enthusiasm.

"More than powerful-showerful, he has very good contacts. Minku's fiancé's family are also bhakts, so Swamiji fixed it all up. Although they don't tell anyone, but I have my sources. I have started going to him regularly now. He has very high-profile bhakts . . . You never know . . ."

My mother has finally found solace in religion

courtesy of my single status. There's an upside to everything.

"Ma, I think Lata Didi wants to say something." I cut short the conversation and hand the phone over to my surprised cousin.

"I hope you are spending the night here . . . unless you have other plans," Lata Didi says later, with a not-so-subtle attempt at intrusiveness.

"No, I have an early-morning shift tomorrow."

"Sure?"

My cousin, like most married people in the "sex only on days that begin with a T" phase of their relationship, is really curious about my love life. I don't know what it is, but married people assume that independent, single people have sex every day of the week. In truth, I am a born-again virgin, and if I give up the booze and the ciggies, I could be up for sainthood.

"In fact, I should leave now."

"Wait, at least eat something. Does your present diet permit sliced watermelons?"

"Only if they've been soaked in vodka." I smile.

I eat the watermelon and vow that this is going to be my dinner. That vow lasts for exactly fifteen minutes as I pull into the neighborhood KFC.

"Welcome back, ma'am." The young man at the counter greets me enthusiastically.

"The number four, and don't supersize it today." Compromises have to be made at times. There is something so comforting in a greasy bag of fries and a crumb-fried burger patty.

As I walk back to the car with the greasy little bag

in my hand, a large Dumpster materializes out of nowhere. When did we start getting those in India? I am always looking for signs and maybe this is it. And just like that, I let go of my beloved greasy bag. I decide then and there that I am going to stop looking for comfort in the wrong places. Boom Voice Raghav will be proud.

The next morning, as I walk into the lobby in my sari, I realize the futility of all diets. The way we are meant to drape this article of clothing, no one will ever notice the change in my figure. I call it the *saas bahu* drape, you know, with the pallav in front and absolutely no skin showing.

There is a buzz in the hotel; one can always tell when something exciting is brewing. You can't talk about it because discretion is the name of the game, but there is certainly something in the air, and it is palpable in the smallest details, from the doorman's stance to the flower arrangements to the color of the receptionist's lipstick. But the one thing that really gives it all away is my boss being visible for once, and not closeted in his love nest.

"Good morning, sir."

"Oh, good morning, Aisha," he replies in a cheery drill sergeant tone.

"What's the matter? Everyone is on full charge."

"Sohail Mustafa is checking in."

"You mean the Pakistani cricketer?" I exclaim excitedly.

"Keep it down, Aisha. Please don't go around

gushing. I don't know what he does to you women," the boss states in exasperation.

"He doesn't do *anything* for me, sir. I need to brief the Reception staff," I say in my most professional voice.

I walk away from the boss and break into a sprint once I am sure I am out of his line of vision. I dash back into the locker room and change my lipstick to a cherry red, re-do my hair into a chignon, and spray on some more perfume. The result is simply irresistible. I do my little kiss face for the mirror. Fine, so I lied, Sohail Mustafa does something to me too.

Unfortunately, he does something for my boss as well, because D.P.G. shadows him from the time he gets down at the main porch all the way to his room. All we get is a glimpse from afar. I go back to my locker and replace the bright red lipstick for a muted one. Maybe another time, I think sadly.

I think someone heard my prayers. I am looking intently into my computer when a deep-throated voice commands my attention. "I need to change some currency." I look up to see the six-foot-three-inch sports hunk smiling at me. Okay, so he is also a married man of a different faith and belongs to a sometimes hostile state. I can see Mama Bhatia having a coronary, but the prospect of being begum number two is extremely appealing. "Miss, I need to change some currency," he repeats.

"Yes, of course, sir." I spring into action. "Please have a seat."

As he parks his firm derriere in the chair, I am in heaven. I avoid staring at him directly and slowly convert his dollars into rupees, carefully laboring over each step. Mission complete, all I need is his signature. His fingers brush against mine as he takes the pen from me. He signs with a flourish and returns the pen to me.

Our fingers touch once more.

No one is ever going to use this pen again. I am going to get one of those strings and hang it around my neck, I decide fiercely.

"Do you need anything else from me?" He flirts. Okay, maybe he only asked, but it seems like flirting to me. *Is he kidding me!*

"No, sir, that will be all. Thank you." I blush, donning my most professional yet feminine avatar.

"May I have my money then?" he asks politely and leans forward ever so slightly. I let out a silent sigh. Here I am thinking I am in jannat or something. I quickly hand over the money and smile idiotically.

A voice cuts in just as I am admiring his receding athletic figure. "Aisha, a little more crispness, please." It is my boss with his usual onion breath and offensive remarks.

One day I will kill him.

On my way out of the Orchid, I decide to collect my medical reimbursement from the accountant. It is the end of the month and I need funding. Unfortunately, it looks like I am not the only one with the same idea. I get into line, and as luck has it, the boss comes and stands right behind me. The last thing I want to do is conduct a conversation with him. There's something about being in a queue: If you happen to be next to someone you know, it's like you are obliged to talk to him or her. Fortunately, his phone rings and I am spared the task of practicing my conversational skills. His conversation continues till I reach the window and I begin to get bored with eavesdropping. He winds up his little chat with a soft "Me too" and a little "Mooaah." With his Bluetooth on, people are likely to think it is a "Mooaah" directed at me. I want to scream.

"I hope you have brought all the proper chemist's bills this time." It's dour-faced Rao. It's amazing how if you pronounce it right, "dour" rhymes with "Rao."

"Yes, Mr. Rao, all twenty-five hundred worth." I am not going to give him the pleasure of deducting my money because of some insignificant formality. In my entire working career, I have never walked away from this window with my due. But today is going to be different. You would think Rao owned the company, the distress he undergoes at being separated from its money. It must be an accountant thing, or maybe it's just him. He is probably cut up about being just a general cashier and not a CA, the penultimate for any number-crunching dude. I try to smile at this evil man but am met with a cold stare.

"Let me see," he says, snatching my bills. Does this man ever smile?

I turn around and acknowledge my boss, but he is busy texting someone.

"Okay, here you are. Two thousand three hundred and eighty rupees." Rao holds out the money.

"Hello, I gave you bills worth two thousand five hundred rupees! Why are you giving me less money?" I demand, all self-righteous. It's not about the money. It's about the principle of it. Even my boss is paying attention now. Too late, I realize that I have been set up by the wily old accountant. His smile is triumphant as he hands me a piece of paper. I finally discover that he does smile and that he has all his teeth.

"You gave a hundred and twenty rupees extra to Sohail Mustafa, my friend. It has to be deducted from you."

I look at the paper, then at Rao, and then at my boss, who looks at me with his usual disapproval.

"You know what," I say, leaning forward and snatching my cash, "it was totally worth it!"

Future, Past, Present

I show Misha the email I found in Karan's apartment the moment she comes over that evening. "Do you think it's stealing?"

"No, it's not an object or anything, he can just make another printout."

"Hmm, I don't know. I feel guilty and stupid."

"Think about it, Aisha. It was a piece of paper lying on the table. What if you had accidentally jotted down a number or something on it and took it with you? How were you to know that it was important?" Misha is one of the most amoral people I know, and sometimes I am grateful for it.

"You're right, Mish."

"What you need to worry about is what you're going to *do* about it."

"Oh, nothing. It's okay... He has never said anything to me. It's not like we're in a relationship...

He kissed me, though. And I must admit it was quite magical."

"There you go. You have to chart your own destiny, which means getting rid of the competition."

"I can do that?"

"Well, we all have this latent streak. You got rid of Tanya, although you did not mean to. You just have to unleash the inner bitch in you. And I mean it in the most complimentary sense."

Tantalizing Tanya left in a huff that night at Karan's party. Apparently, she was very upset to find me passed out on Karan's bed. Karan was very amused. This, of course, is all Misha's version as I was dead to the world of the sober and sensible.

"I don't know if I have an inner bitch in me."

"We all do, darling. Don't worry, he's not going anywhere."

I begin to feel upbeat again, but Misha seems pensive and with good reason. The marriage market is obviously buoyant. Why then are we the only ones facing a scarcity? She plonks herself next to me on the sofa and grabs my ciggie. I light another one. "You think he's bride hunting here?" I ask, desperate for it to be untrue.

"Possibly, but now that he has you, I'm sure he's not looking."

"You think?"

"Of course. It's so obvious," Misha responds confidently. Just one more reason why she is my best friend: She has the ability to reinforce all the thoughts I am too chicken to put into words. "This should prove to you that there is no merit in being such a puritan. That's why you're still single. Always treading the straight line."

"And just how far have your manipulations taken you?"

"Well, I've met someone," she says with a smile.

"Who?"

"The guy at the party, remember?"

"My recollections of the party are very blurred," I admit truthfully.

"Oh, I forgot," Misha says and winks at me. "He's a banker and supercute. Very gentlemanly and witty, and we are going to go out again soon."

"Does the supercute banker have a name?"

"Yes, it's Sharad Mahadik."

Now, why does that name sound so familiar?

The niece of one of Karan's important clients is getting married and he calls to ask if I would personally assist with the wedding preparations at the Grand Orchid. Of course, I comply sweetly, but in truth, I am ready to go ballistic. I'm not kidding you, weddings drive me crazy . . . absolutely loco. It's not like I have some philosophical stand against them. (That is the case only with Valentine's Day. On that one day of the year I'm a Shiv Sena sympathizer. They're a right-wing political party with a strong emphasis on the Hindu way and an aversion to all things "Western.") I'm speaking exclusively of weddings that take place in my hotel. Every single employee in the hotel hates them for the crassness of the rowdy guests, the spill of flower petals and butter chicken, and the mental distress they cause to all those involved, especially me.

I spend a week fixing up the honeymoon suite. Typically, the "marriage party" wants it all, and typically we have our "policies," the most contentious of all being the issue of sprinkling rose petals on the bridal bed. It's a huge no-no. Rose petals when crushed under writhing bodies irreparably stain the sheets, and the Grand Orchid can't have that. I am embroiled in this stand-off between romance and hotel policy, with the housekeeper baying for my blood. The other issue is of candles. "Only two per room," I have been told. We cannot have too many flammable items in the room. This leads to another battle between the marriage party and the management. I idiotically go to D. P. Gupta for support under a "let me check with my manager" ruse, only to be turned away at the door to his office. "Aisha, it's not the first damn wedding we have had in the hotel. Handle it!" Right, handle it. They can have the bloody candles, even if it means that I spend the night outside the bridal chamber armed with a fire extinguisher in my hands.

The engagement, a day prior to the wedding, is to take place on the hotel lawn, and I scurry around at the last minute to ensure that everything is in place.

The whole marriage business gets a little better when Karan asks me to be his date that evening. We are not walking down any red carpet, but it is his client's niece's engagement party. And soon the pressure of being seen with him at a traditional official do begins to mount. It starts innocently enough with what I should wear, and then I go from wondering about how to conduct myself to what he is going to introduce me as to whether we should talk about the kiss. Misha is probably the only one who can solve this dilemma.

"I think he'll say 'This is my friend, Aisha.' What do you think, Misha?" I ask her over the phone.

"No, he'll probably say 'girlfriend.'"

"*Girlfriend* is so high school. We are not teenagers. You can't say 'girlfriend' anymore, it's so cheesy!"

"Maybe he'll say 'my lover.' So continental." Misha giggles.

"Or partner . . ."

"Too gay. Let's just wait and see. So, once again, what are you going to wear?"

"I should wear a sari, but then, on the other hand, I'm not really part of the wedding, you know. I'm part of the management. Maybe I can wear westerns."

"No, you have to wear a sari, come on. Play the part."

"Okay, but a sari makes me look fat."

"Not if you drape it right."

"Okay. But you have to help me, please. And I don't really have a sari to wear."

"I can give you one."

"I'll ask Anu. Thanks for your offer, but I need a sari, not a sarong. Yours are so tiny they'd only half cover me. So what's the news with Mr. Sharad

Maha-dick?" I ask, feeling that I should take as much interest in her love life as she has in mine.

"Well, he does a lot of international conference calls, and then I can't reach him, and it's always in the evenings. So annoying, really."

"I suppose he has a demanding career . . ."

"Very demanding. He works most weekends."

"So when do you meet?"

"During the week, for dinner. It's always supremely romantic. He does the whole flower thing too. The other day I was out when he sent me this huge bouquet of orchids."

"So he's stingy with his time but not his money. Better than Samir or Cheap Deep."

"Please, don't even compare the two."

True, there is no comparison between them. I'll go with the money any day. God, dating is so expensive, and not just for men. With men, it's all the obvious costs like gas bills and dinner bills, etc. With women there are so many hidden costs—new clothes, regular salon visits, waxing your legs, doing your eyebrows, coloring your hair, new shoes . . . We do all these things anyway, but when you start seeing someone you really like, the frequency and intensity multiply. Unfortunately, your income doesn't. These days you can get a loan for almost anything, but not, alas, for designer wear. Life is just not fair. I would choose a Swarovski-encrusted sari over a washing machine any day. And, believe me, I am not the only one who feels that way.

———

Misha keeps her word and comes over to help me drape the national garment. She is ingenious and I discover that it is possible for me to wear a sari and have a waist. She pins the pleats together with a crystal brooch that sits strategically below my belly button. It is, of course, covered by the pallav but sparkles seductively through the sheerness of the fabric. I am not sure whether drawing attention to my belly is the smartest fashion statement, but it is my day for taking chances. My blouse has sleeves, much to Misha's disappointment, but other than that, she is as pleased with the results as I am. At this point, at the risk of sounding like one of those promo plugs, let me add that the outfit is courtesy of my very generous friend Anushka from her mothballed wedding trousseau.

"I think he's here," I say at the sound of the door-bell.

I am disappointed to see the driver at the door. The sahib is apparently waiting in the car. I am a little old-fashioned in these matters. I feel that the guy should come to the door when he comes to pick you up, and drop you off as well; it's basic etiquette. It's only gangsters who send their honchos or chauffeurs to pick up their molls.

As these thoughts whirl around in my head, I see Karan leaning against the car. He is on the phone and looking straight at me. I suddenly grow terribly self-conscious. This is the worst part of a new relationship. At this stage, all emphasis is on the physical appearance—"the walk" is of utmost importance. How much you enjoy being the center of attention depends entirely on your opinion about yourself. Once you're past stealing surreptitious glances, you can enter the "I can now look at you openly" phase of the relationship. Except that I am still not ready for the open stare. *Please God, don't let me trip.*

I try to minimize the duration of "the walk" and reach Karan in one piece and in record time.

Karan breaks his stare with a smile. "You look great! The sari really suits you." *It must be love, or he is going blind!*

"Really, it's been so last minute. A really crazy day . . ." I lie with alarming ease.

A lot of money has been spent on the do. Flowers of every variety adorn the facade and are prettily fashioned in a sign of welcome. My touch is everywhere. A long winding pathway shaded by a vine trellis leads us into the Garden of Eden. I ensured that the tattered red or green carpets that used to be de rigueur at these marriage thingies were classily replaced with the real thing: verdant green grass. You know, the real stuff that comes rolled like a carpet. Of course, I had a near altercation with the landscaper and had to assure him that the lawn wouldn't be ruined. It feels good to sink my stilettos into the grass. Gentle piped music floats around us instead of screeching shehnais. The food is perfect. My seasoned eye tries to follow the stewards as they carry out the trays of caviar, but my line of vision is blocked by the liveried waiters who pass by with flutes of Moët & Chandon, while others hold out silver salvers of oysters nestled in beds of crushed ice. I beam at them and nod in approval.

As Karan and I wind our way through this maze of gastronomic delights, I promise myself that if I am to ever have an engagement party, this is how I will do it. Even better.

"There's Mr. Sinha, let's go over to him," Karan says, looking into the sea of people.

I look at the blue-suited man who is Karan's client and heaven help me, it is none other than "Sinful Sin-ha." "Is that him with the comb-over?"

"Aisha," Karan chides, "he's losing his hair, be nice."

Sin-ha is a regular guest or rather an abomination at the hotel. S.S., as we call him at work, is the kind of sleaze who only conducts conversations with certain parts of the anatomy . . . I think you get the drift. You can imagine my surprise when he looks at my face and recognizes me.

"Hello, Karan, hello, Aisha. You've done a great job. The place looks absolutely extraordinary!" he says, extending his hand.

"Thank you, Mr. Sinha." I smile back. *Don't you dare drop your gaze.*

"Have you met the happy couple? Let me take you to them." I walk along, very aware of Sinha's greasy hand on my arm. And then, as the crowd parts to make way for the uncle of the bride, the podium comes into view, and my world starts to move in slow motion. Amid the hybrid blooms of this artificial Garden of Eden, I catch a glimpse of a very real hell. Standing right there at the receiving end of a queue of well-wishers is the ex, very real and very handsome, and in the sherwani I had helped him pick out during one of our shopping sprees.

I have dreamt of this moment so often and here it is, very real, exactly as I envisioned it, with one minor change: a different bride. If there is a hell on earth, this has to be it. My feet feel like lead and each step is an excruciating effort. As I take in the details of the sight in front of me, I can't help but feel a sense of betrayal like never before. Not only has my ex gotten engaged without telling me, he and his betrothed are bedecked in matching Shantanu and Nikhil creations! A double whammy.

Why hadn't I paid more attention and tried to find out at least the names of the bride and groom, instead of obsessing over trivialities, like grass versus carpet?

The queue to the "happy couple" suddenly seems too short and I quickly resolve to play the bon vivant even if it kills me. I grit my teeth and join the line with a radiant expression firmly in place. Why am I feeling awkward when I am walking up to the ex with a gorgeous man at my side? I look like quite a dish myself. I am glad I wore the sari after all.

We are just three people away, but the ex has not spotted me. Karan is deep in conversation with S.S. He turns and smiles at me. Is that a reassuring smile? Has he noticed my moral dilemma? My face begins to hurt from the fake smile. This is the wrong time to switch expressions. Everything is in a very delicate balance. And God is really in the details.

At this inopportune moment, the heel of my

stiletto gets firmly lodged between two boards that make up the podium. Sheer negligence, coupled with my fragile emotional state of mind, is what leads to this major distress. S.S. and Karan are on the verge of greeting the happy couple. I try to extricate my heel by doing an awkward little twist, but to no avail. I am suddenly acutely aware of the long, winding queue of people behind me. I can hear discreet mumblings and I can sense the impatience. After all, I am delaying everyone's sprint to the buffet. I stand there helpless with a stupid grin on my face. Fortunately, the over-helpful, and possibly famished, aunty behind me notices the cause of my distress.

Before we proceed, here's a little dish on these women. They are ubiquitous at weddings, receptions, rokas (the most important first step in the multitiered extravaganzas that are our weddings, where you "reserve" your groom or bride, but can still change your mind), etc. You can find them lurking everywhere, but the two most likely places are the buffet counter and at a respectable twenty-foot distance from the bar, far enough to appear decent and yet close enough to keep a tight rein on their husbands. The aunties, however, are kindness personified and the first volunteers to fix your drooping pallu, the fold of the sari that covers the bosom, either with a look or by taking matters into their own hands. They are also aces at multitasking by effectively training their X-ray vision on your drink for the evening and mentally analyzing its contents. Like FBI operatives on a sting operation, they usually stake out weddings and other such social gatherings. These aunties, unlike some of the uncles, look at you unabashedly, and if in a group, then several pairs of eyes are fixed on you in amazing synchronization. I assume it must be like facing a firing squad, except this one challenges you to smile at them, which you must do, especially if you are a single gal. You never know whose mommy or maasi one of them could turn out to be.

"Stand still, I will bend and pull it out," the aunty offers charitably.

"Thank you so much."

At this point Karan and S.S. reach the happy couple. And I remain stuck in this embarrassing predicament.

"Uff . . . this is stuck badly. Chottu, go in front and pull Aunty from the other side." She addresses a guy who doen't look like a chottu. He must be at least nineteen years old.

Chottu takes both my arms and begins to pull. "I'm really not that old," I state unnecessarily.

"I know," he breathes, holding me a little too close. *Shit, Chottu is a lech!*

At this point, during this human tug of war, the happy couple and Karan turn around to see what the commotion is all about. Voilà, it's me, the cynosure of all eyes. To make matters worse, neither the ex nor Karan looks surprised. It's the bride-to-be who looks shocked. I stumble toward Karan with my heel successfully extricated and my pride bruised by repeated manhandling.

"Are you okay?" Karan asks.

"Fine." That question is one of his favorite phrases. It has come to be a standard feature in our relationship and it is totally not cool.

"Aisha, meet the happy couple." S.S. finally makes the introductions.

The ex really does look happy. Frankly, if I were wearing Shantanu and Nikhil, I would be ecstatic too, no matter whom I was getting engaged to. But his expression changes when he sees me.

"Group photograph, please," S.S. suggests.

"Of course," I chime in over-brightly. "Congratulations on your big day," I say, keeping my eyes resolutely on the girl and completely ignoring the ex. *He sucks in bed,* I want to whisper.

Of course, I don't say any such thing. I proceed to pose for a photograph that is definitely meant for posterity. Misha is right. This is all live theater. All of us play our part by quelling spontaneity to put on the garb of civility. We appear empowered in order to hide our failures, or vulnerable when it serves the purpose. In the end, it all comes to zip.

But one thing that does count at an engagement or wedding party at a five-star hotel is the plate count at the buffet. When the busy manager at the end of the evening presents a bill to the weary marriage party, his means of justifying the charge is the number of plates used. And so I stoop to a level that only an ex can inspire in one. I proceed to take a separate plate for every bite I eat, and sometimes even for the ones I don't.

Karan watches me quietly as I toss plate after barely used plate into an eager waiter's hands.

"Allow me," he finally says as I am about to hand over the eighteenth. "So, how do you know him?" he asks, leading me away from the buffet.

"Who, Sin-ful?" I ask indifferently.

"No," he says patiently, "the groom."

"I nearly married him," I say after a brief pause.

Karan finally looks surprised and there is a second of pin-drop silence. "Aisha, I'm so sorry. I wouldn't have put you through this if I'd known."

"It's okay, it was a long time ago."

"Is it long enough?" Karan stares pensively into the distance.

I turn to face him and utter what I have known for some time now. "Yes, it is."

"How about we find another party, then?" he says, taking my hand with a disarming smile, the relief shining in his eyes.

"Yes, I think I'm about finished here." I finally start to relax. "By the way, do you know your business acquaintance is a big-time sleaze?"

"Aisha..." Karan says, laughing, "we haven't even left the party."

Boys Do Cry

We leave that sorry soirée for the Polo Club. Karan finds us a quiet table that overlooks the lush lawns. I take in the crisp night air and finally begin to relax. We are in the middle of a comforting Armagnac when a couple walks up to our table. The guy looks vaguely familiar, but I just can't place him. That's another issue with working in hotels: Your brain is overloaded with having to store faces and names, and more often than not, faces without names.

"Aisha, this is Sharad and his wife, Veena." Karan introduces us.

"We met at the housewarming party. I don't think Aisha remembers much of that night." Sharad laughs.

It all comes back to me in a flash. This is the obscene guy who came on to me on the terrace the night of Karan's party. He looks much better in moonlight. In the cove lighting of the Polo Club, he is just one of those greasy, light-eyed, fair-skinned, *icky* guys.

"So, Veena, sorry to have missed you at the party."

"I know, I was traveling for work. Hope Sharad was a good boy."

One word out of Veena and you know that she is the one who wears the pants.

I had a male colleague who once said that women bosses could be placed at two ends of the spectrum, either Ma, the mother, or Chandi Ma, the embodiment of the Goddess Kali at her most wrathful. At the time, I found the statement appalling, but looking at Veena, I know exactly where the needle stopped with her. She is one of those stereotypical hard-nosed, multinational working women. I actually feel sorry for Sharad as he stands timidly behind her.

"How do you know them?" I ask Karan after they leave.

"I met them at a party when I first got here. Imagine, they'll have been married five years tomorrow. They must have married young."

"Must have . . ."

Veena handed me her visiting card as a parting shot with a "Let's meet up sometime." What kind of person uses her visiting card as a means of social introduction? I glance down at this new tablet of cool, and there lies the answer. The vice president of a large consumer goods kind of outfit would do that sort of thing. Veena Prasad-Mahadik. So she is also among the new breed of women who hold on to their maiden name and hyphenate it with the husband's last name. It's supposed to be the cool way to tell the world you're married, but frankly, I feel it makes them sound more like a firm of chartered accountants.

You don't need to be a rocket scientist to figure out just what's going on. Our friend Sharad Mahadik is Misha's new boyfriend. Rather, he is Misha's new *married* boyfriend. I feel a twist in my stomach and a strange heat creeping up behind my ears.

"Aisha, are you okay?" Karan breaks my train of thought.

"Will you stop asking me that all the time?" I snap.

Karan looks taken aback and I am truly embarrassed. I did not mean to be rude to him. I can't think of anything constructive to say. "Can we call it a night, Karan? I have an early day tomorrow."

"Yeah, maybe it's all been too much," he says pointedly.

I don't respond and the rest of the evening passes in silence. I get out of his car and walk into my building. He does not see me to the door. This is not the way the evening was supposed to end. Karan was not supposed to believe that I am still stuck on my ex. But if this is the price I have to pay for preserving my friend's reputation, then it's worth it.

———

"Mish, I'm sorry to wake you." The first thing I do after closing the door upon arrival is call Misha.

"Everything okay? The sari didn't come undone or something?"

"No, everything held up great. Including me. Guess whose party it was?"

"I'm half asleep, just tell me."

"The ex's engagement."

"Okay, now I'm awake, so tell me all."

It's not easy breaking bad news to anyone, even if she is one of your best friends. I did it once before, to confirm Anushka's suspicions about Anuj, and now it is poor Misha's turn.

Misha arrives at my house bright and early at seven in the morning. She probably didn't get much sleep after our conversation the previous night. And I feel the onslaught of a full-blown flu. I am burning up and I feel like my head is about to explode.

"My turn to wake you up," she says cheerfully.

"Be my guest," I croak.

"You look like hell. What happened? Is Karan married as well?"

"He will be one day, but not to me."

"It went badly?"

I wave her question aside. "I have the flu. I'm not going to work today."

"Let me make you some tea and then I want to hear everything. You can talk, right?

"So, the wife's a tough one?" Misha asks, taking in everything I have just told her. "That's perfect for what I have in mind."

"Misha, what happened to graceful exits? Forewarned is forearmed—that kind of stuff."

"He led me on, Aisha, that's wrong. Do you know I nearly slept with him!"

"You never told me that."

"Well...because it was an awkward experience."

"You're not getting away with that. You have to tell me."

We plonk ourselves on the bed. I snuggle under the blanket and Misha decides to tell all. Apparently her relationship with Sharad got off to a roaring start. It was lust at first sight for them both, more action and less conversation. Sharad was sexy and romantic and their dates were always interspersed with flowers and kisses. Although it was moving very fast, she never felt like she was being pushed into anything. She was being wooed like never before. He had restrictions because of his demanding job, but they managed to spend quality time together. He really did make every minute count.

A few days ago, after a dinner date, probably when the wife was traveling, Sharad and Misha found themselves in each other's arms. They were in the elevator up to her apartment and he did one of those hitched-up-against-the-wall numbers...very passionate and breathless. (Luckily, Mrs. Mukherjee was away visiting a friend in Kolkata.) They stumbled out of the elevator and straight into the apartment, where they began to disrobe with fervent passion. A trail of clothes marked their hurried passage into the boudoir, and after a session of heavy petting and panting, they were on the verge of what is called going all the way. (I don't know why it's called that, I got stuck with the phrase in college just like the rest of you.) Anyhow, at that point, he stopped, just like that. It was terribly awkward, but Misha also felt strangely relieved. She did not pursue the matter with him and they called it a night. What could she have done anyway? She put the whole thing down to the easier alternative of performance anxiety. It happens sometimes. Far too many men believe that the ultimate test of manhood is their performance in bed and that they have to ace it every time.

Truth be told, the pressure on men has never been greater than it is today. Battery-operated devices have an unfair advantage these days. It's just not a level playground anymore. Boys do cry sometimes. Let's be honest here: Today when women say *dil-do* they are not speaking in Hindi and they are definitely not asking for your heart!

Anyway, Sharad went home a crushed man that day, and Misha is sure he will welcome any chance to regain his lost title. She is going to give him that opportunity.

———

Misha calls Sharad and arranges for an afternoon rendezvous. She opts for a hotel this time. "It will be a mood enhancer, darling," she purrs, firing herself up to play the queen of seduction.

Nothing is more risqué than a little tryst on your lunch break. Misha begins her game of seduction with the present day's answer to foreplay: the mobile phone.

"Right, I think I've sharpened my texting skills enough." Misha finally puts away her phone. She then picks up Veena Prasad-Mahadik's visiting card and issues directives to me. "I want you to call her when I give you a missed call."

Misha leaves my house at noon for her afternoon tryst with Sharad. She calls at one to say that Sharad is expected at any moment and that I should call his wife in fifteen minutes.

"That's all the time you need?" I am a little anxious. Suppose the plan backfires?

"I have a feeling that even that may be too long. Remember, with him every minute counts." She laughs.

Sharad arrives at the hotel at one, armed with a bouquet of flowers and a bottle of wine. It is not Sula.

"Happy anniversary," Misha coos. Sharad looks taken aback. "It's been forty-one days since we met, silly." She watches him visibly relax and feels her anger rise. But this is not the moment for emotion of any kind.

"There's such a thing as a forty-one-day anniversary?" Sharad asks.

"I'm a happy girl, I like celebrating things," Misha says, wrapping her arms around Sharad. She shuts the door firmly behind her and leads him to the bed. She takes a look at him and relishes the vision of the moment and is almost tempted to forgo the plan and snuggle up next to him. But she crosses that thought from her head; there are some things that a girl just won't do. "Let me switch off my mobile phone, I don't want us to be disturbed for the next hour." She takes the opportunity to ring me and quickly hang up so that a missed call appears on my phone.

I am parked outside a PCO and go into the little store to make the call. *Is this what adult relationships are all about?*

"Madam, local call or STD?" the clerk asks between puffs of beedi.

"Local." *Someone tell me how this makes a difference.*

"Madam, then use a pay phone, not a booth." He educates me in PCO etiquette—apparently their facilities are only meant for the long-distance calls in addition to faxes and emailing. The sign on the yellow phone says: ONE RUPEE COIN. "New rupee coin only," he continues, barely glancing up at me, his head bent over a tattered magazine.

This is great, it just gets easier and easier. I dig my hands into my pockets. I find a new one-rupee coin and pop it in the slot. This is not Vegas and that ain't no slot machine. The hideous yellow monster eats my coin and an automated voice reprimands me first in English and then in Hindi as I try to dial out. I begin to feel desperate; I am running out of time.

"*Bhaiyyaji, bahut* urgent phone *karna hai.*"

"Mobile *ki* landline?" the clerk asks, finally looking up and warming to the urgency in my voice.

"Mobile."

"*Pehle batana tha. Phife rupees lagenge.*"

I accept his terms—five rupees; I should have told him earlier the call was to a cell phone—and dash back into the booth, immediately getting down to business. I reclaim my somewhat foreign accent and call the Mrs. and follow Misha's instructions. I hang up hoping that she will take the call seriously. The task over, I go home and get back into bed and wait for Misha to call.

The timing is perfect. After the anonymous phone call, the Mrs. telephones her philandering hubby, who at that moment is in the shower. Misha answers the phone and then discreetly hangs up in response to the "Who's speaking" snapped at her. She has already prepared for what is to ensue. She gathers up Sharad's discarded clothes and puts them in a bag with his mobile phone. A carefully picked-out floral anniversary card is strategically placed on the table. The telephone wires in the room have already been disconnected. "I'll join you in a minute, darling," Misha calls out to the man in the shower as she carefully exits, double-locking the door on her way out.

———

"He's toast." I am anxiously awaiting her call.

"Where are you?"

"In the lobby."

"Leave, madwoman! Why do you want drama?"

"I have to see how it ends. Besides, the wife doesn't know me. And I doubt that Sharad will acknowledge me even if he does see me."

I give Misha a description of Mrs. Mahadik and she quickly hangs up on spotting her. The wife heads straight for the elevator. She is down in five minutes; clearly, she didn't manage to get him to open the door. The lobby manager then follows her back up to the room. Great, the audience is expanding.

Misha ensured the removal of all towels, bathrobes, and bedding before check-in. "I get a terrible rash, so I always carry my own," she told the receptionist while making the reservation. So poor Sharad is left dripping wet and buck naked. In his hand is the anniversary card from Misha that acknowledges their forty-one-day anniversary. He is obliged to be grateful for her last thoughtful gesture though, for when the door to his room opens, he does have something to conceal his nakedness with. And, yes, for those of you who insist on the greasy details, it isn't a very big card.

Fifteen minutes later Mrs. Mahadik returns to the lobby with a shamefaced man in a bathrobe following four steps behind. They go to settle the bill at Reception.

"They're at Reception . . . I'm going to walk past him," Misha whispers to me over the phone.

"Let it be, Mish." When it comes to confrontation, I really am a wimp.

But Misha is reveling in her victory. She sashays past a bathrobe-clad Sharad, catches his eye, and gives him an audacious wink. And you thought this stuff only happens in the movies.

The Big "S"

*I*t looks like the ex's search for true love has finally come to an end. He calls soon after the engagement party. He claims that he didn't feel it necessary to *burden* me with the details of his love life as we had all moved on with our lives. Maybe he is right, but there is always plain old curiosity.

"Don't you want to know who I was with that night?" I challenge.

"Karan. Sinha Uncle has some business dealings with him."

"You're always so glib. Weren't you surprised to find me with this gorgeous man?"

"Aisha, your definition of a 'gorgeous man' leaves much to be desired. And they are usually gay. So, what do you want me to say?"

I hang up.

It is time for me to bury the past and focus on the

future. I don't want to lose out on Karan. I left him thinking that I wasn't over the ex. I have to make him see the truth.

It's officially the wedding season, nestled auspiciously between Diwali and Christmas. Most of the people I know are already married or are far from it, so there aren't too many such events penciled in my diary. This, of course, is discounting the accidental invite to the ex's engagement bash.

I feel a little embarrassed at having allowed my feelings about my earlier failed relationship to show quite so openly. Karan is beginning to consume my thoughts a lot more than I am ready to admit. I just am not up for another disappointment.

I call him that night, but the conversation is strained. I can sense that I have pushed him away. We exchange pleasantries, but we are both distinctly aware of the strain between us.

"Aisha, it's okay if you need some time out. Maybe we have been spending too much time together."

"I thought that was the idea, spending time together, getting to know each other."

"I know . . . but one has to be ready."

"But I am ready."

"Maybe I'm not ready, Aisha."

"Oh," I say, the implication suddenly striking home. "Is this your way of telling a girl that you've had enough of her?"

"Look, that's not true. Don't overreact. Let's meet up sometime next week or something..."

It sounds like a sympathy meeting to me. If he wants the big S—i.e., space—then he will have it.

"Yes...whatever." I try to hide my disappointment and appear just as vague.

Women have a reputation for being complicated and hard to understand. I think that's a lazy approach. The silent and highly underestimated communication buster is the male ego. I assume that women who are either engaged, married, or involved do a nifty juggle between their mate's ego and libido. We gals who are single foolishly focus on one more than the other. I, of course, am keeping track of neither. So I guess the big S it will have to be.

It's two days since my last conversation with Karan. I am bedridden all day. The conversation with him has obviously exacerbated my flu. The temptation to call consumes me all day long, but I hold out admirably. The boss is surprisingly understanding about my ill health. He even offers to send across some sick food from the hotel, which I promptly decline. Sick food does exactly that, it makes you feel really sick.

Misha descends on me all gloating and glowing post her victorious encounter. I know that the high is going to be short-lived. But I am certainly not going to ruin this moment for her.

"You should have seen them in the lobby. I

wish I could have been there when she opened the door."

"I'm glad it's behind you, really. Next time, just be careful."

"There is no next time now, I'm going to get married."

"What? When?"

"I'm thinking March," Misha replies confidently.

"I'm confused. What are you doing? Setting a date and working backward?"

"Something like that. I never got off that desivivaha.com. In fact, I logged on to two more . . ."

"And you never told me."

"Tell you and endure a gyaan session?"

Endure a gyaan session . . . Do we all really grow up to be our mothers, always lecturing others?

Misha is right in wanting to give up her search for the one true love. There is no guarantee that the digital world will throw up a suitable option, but at least when you find someone on the net, you know he has marriage on his mind.

I think there is a point in everyone's life when the search for Mr. Right is reduced to the search for Mr. Right Now. A desperate attempt at fleeing loneliness often results in fleeting relationships. It's at this point that we get all fatalistic about love and adopt the *que sera sera* attitude. Perhaps there is something to working backward by first setting a date and then proceeding to look for a potential mate. Apart from everything else, we all work better with a deadline.

Misha hooks up the laptop while I sip my

Batchelors mulligatawny soup. Rather sexist branding, if you ask me. Anyway, let's not get into advertising and stereotyping and fairness creams. I should just be grateful that it's not called Spinster's. That would really plunge me into the depths of despair.

Online spouse-hunting is actually a lot of fun once you get into it. It's like an electronic swayamvar— traditional Hindu speed-dating when princesses chose their grooms from a row of men. Except it's a customized swayamvar. It does have its own stomach-knotting moments, especially once you have expressed an interest in someone and are waiting for a response. It takes guts to put yourself out there, if you ask me.

"No one that I've expressed an interest in has responded," Misha says, clearly disappointed. She props herself against a pillow and frowns intently at the screen.

"Don't worry, it takes time." I try to console her, but I can see that it is not working.

The new website is quite effective, but it is an arduous process. It should really have been designed like a Google search, where you just put in your key words—for example, *tall, handsome, six-figure salary, ripped body*—and find your match.

"Please, where's the fun in that?" she says, dismissing my clever idea.

"Well ... it would make things so much easier. ..."

"I guess you're right, Aisha." My friends and I can go to imaginative lengths in search of a perfect mate; we are equally good at finding new ways of feeling insecure.

We quickly start to scroll through the profiles of the contending females. And then we chance upon an eerily familiar profile.

It is mine. The rest is a blur.

As we scroll through my details, I am further horrified. Not only am I on this blessed website, but I have been described as "large framed."

"Misha, I thought I asked you to take me off this!"

"Aisha, I never put you on this one. You were on desivivaha—"

"Please..."

"Aisha, I would never call you 'large framed.' Never." She looks at me as if I have injured her sensibilities. True, Misha would never call me "large framed." That would be a huge breach of trust! "Look, Aisha, it says it's been posted by a guardian or parent."

I can't believe it. On the top right-hand corner, it states that the profile had been created and posted one month ago by a parent or guardian. It can't be Mama Bhatia. She isn't net savvy. Or is she? I haven't been home in nearly a year. Things could have changed. I wonder if this is where the pyaaz-garlic guy suddenly emerged from. After all, marriage proposals through family connections diminished after four years in the big city and completely ceased once I crossed the twenty-five benchmark.

There is only one way to find out. I dial my mother and tell Misha to remain silent in the background. If my mother discovers that I'm going ballistic in front of an audience, I will be apologizing to her for the rest of my life. I am permitted to be rude, but only in private. I have, after all, been raised with some samskara—some values.

"Hello, beta." My mother answers in one ring. She is in some place where the incessant peal of bells is deafening. "You called at such an auspicious time. I am at Swami Raman's . . ."

"How can you hear the phone in that racket?"

"It was on vibrating mode, beta." If my mother can figure out the vibrating mode on her mobile phone, she can log on to the net for sure.

"Ma, I need to speak to you. Can you just step out for a minute?"

"Okay, one moment."

I hold on patiently as my mother excuses her way through a seemingly busy and fervent throng. As the sound of the bells recedes, the certainty of my mother's involvement intensifies.

"Ma, have you registered me on a marriage web-site?" I ask, getting straight to the point.

"Why do you ask?"

"Now, Ma, I want to know the truth. I am being very serious here."

"Yes, I did, beta," my mother says, rising to the challenge. Aggression is not the right way of dealing with my mother, especially when she is convinced that her fight is for a just cause.

"I am so disappointed in you for not telling me," I say in an injured tone, "and you called me 'large framed' in the profile. . . ."

"Beta, you have to be honest about these things." Her tone softens.

"But you haven't seen me in a year, a lot has changed."

"Maybe, but better to be cautious in these matters. After a certain age, especially for a girl living alone . . . There are a lot of challenges . . ."

"Like what?" I can feel the resentment setting in. Trust my mother to look at being independent and socially active as a handicap.

"Well, you know boys like fresh girls . . ."

"Fresh! What are we talking about, vegetables? What's with you and marriage and food groups?"

"*Fresh* girls, you know . . ." My mother continues awkwardly.

"Oh, please, just say virgins. Why is that so hard?"

"Please don't talk like that!" she snaps.

" 'Fresh' is the most vulgar thing I have ever heard," I sputter, realizing a little too late that I have crossed the line.

"Anyway, I am in a place of worship. I will not take any more stress in my life."

I slam the phone down on her. Actually, I think it is a rather synchronized reaction.

Mama Mía...
Here We Go Again

*K*aran leaves for Mumbai and I concentrate on work. I do so with the admirable enthusiasm of a thulla opting for a night shift during the holiday drinking season. The boss seems particularly pleased to see me and promptly leaves early that evening. I guess he was compelled to work the last couple of days as ol' faithful Rajat was unwell. If you are the "chosen one" and you fail to make an appearance during a busy period, it is nothing short of treachery. No such pressure on me!

I quickly settle into the comfort of being queen for a day. Just three days to go until Karan's return. Yeah, I am doing the countdown bit. Things between us are still in limbo, but my indisposition has given me ample time to reflect and come to the decision that the situation needs to be resolved. Besides, I am already beginning to miss him.

I sit down at my desk and look at the pile of papers I have to go through when my eye falls on a tear sheet that I have neatly folded into my planner. It is one of those questionnaire thingies from one of those chick magazines. This one has a bold heading: "Should You Quit Your Job?" I think about that every day, but the questionnaire has to wait. I make my way to the receptionist's desk as I need to be updated on what has been going on during my absence.

I lean over and whisper, "So, what's been happening, Rish old boy?" Rishi is the in-house gossip mill.

"Miss Lekha is checking in today," Rishi trills. "Sweetie, she is such a 'diva.'"

"I think she's fat!" Seema, our resident beauty queen and public relations lady, joins us. Check-in by any halfway decent-looking female is always competition for this self-elected resident beauty queen of the hotel.

"Oh, you're just jealous. Besides, women with a little meat on them look good. More cushion for the pushin', like my mama used to say," Rishi shoots back.

"Oh, please! How would you know?" Seema stomps off, her hips swinging dangerously from side to side and her high heels clinking against the marble floor. The bellboys sigh as they follow her rapidly retreating derriere. I silence them with a mock serious look.

"Your mother actually said that?" I turn to Rishi. What kind of impact does a statement like that have on a fledgling fairy? Maybe a lifelong devotion to overweight women and alcohol.

"No, she didn't. Figure of speech. Always blame everything on Mommy. Aisha, you have to look at Miss Lekha's list of requirements. Movie stars, I tell you!" He is looking at a piece of paper in his hand.

"Show," I say eagerly. Rishi and I are gossip buddies, and together we pore over the list.

"She needs mineral water, only Evian, and yes, Evian spray as well. Goose-down pillows ... eight of them, not two, not three, but eight."

"Hang on, she needs forty-seven wooden hangers. How many nights is she staying?"

"Two."

"Wooden hangers! Do they have to be Burmese teak?" I ask sarcastically.

"Spider orchids only for flowers ... Moët on ice at all times ... Calls to be screened ... Incognito status ... Macrobiotic diet, only the chef to take her orders ... Bulbs to be at a specified wattage only ..."

"Stop, I can't hear anymore, I want to cry," I squeal.

"Oh, honey, I know. Maybe in another life," Rishi commiserates.

"No, silly, I don't want her life. I just don't want to be on shift when she checks in!" I moan at the prospect of standing for hours with a garland of marigolds in my hand. This visit is sure to put the boss into overdrive.

"Anyway, I have to run, the pool needs my attention," Rishi says in an officious tone. He winks at me and walks away.

"The pool?" I call out after him.

"Did I say pool? Sorry, it's time for that soccer team from Brazil to hit the pool. They might need some help with their thongs. Did you know men from Brazil wear thongs? Bye, bye, Speedos."

I chuckle silently and look around. Everything seems in place. The carpets still feel a bit wet after the shampoo, but they will dry by the end of the day. Then I spot the doorman letting out a big yawn. I will have to do something about that.

As I make my way back to my desk, the phone rings. It's Karan.

"Hi." I am so happy to hear the sound of his voice. He must have been in Mumbai maybe two hours. This is great, he was thinking of me. *I thought he needed space!*

"Aisha, I hope I'm not disturbing you."

"No, not at all. I thought you said you needed space. . . ." I tease gently.

"Changing one's mind is not a woman's prerogative."

"Touché."

"I need to ask for a huge favor."

Just like a man. He needs something, so he's called; how predictable!

"Yes . . . anything. Tell me." And so he does.

Advice to all those who are still reading this book: "Anything" is a blanket term that must be used sparingly, as I am doomed to find out. The favor involves picking up Gucci Mama—aka Karan's mother—from the airport. She was meant to arrive in Delhi from London a couple of weeks later but advanced her visit to avoid the Christmas rush. She is getting in tomorrow and Karan will not be able to make it back in time. So can I help out? Pick her up and get her a room in my hotel for the night?

I had thought of ways in which to show that I cared, but more like picking *him* up from the airport, or going to *his* apartment and watering *his* plants, or maybe even feeding the fish. These are simple, harmless gestures, not potentially life-and-relationship-threatening maneuvers. Love, at the best of times, can be described as an adventure sport, but I am thinking more on the lines of bungee-jumping and not free-falling. But it's too late to back out now.

I get to work the next day and prepare for Gucci Mama's arrival. A room is booked in my hotel. Status: check. Wine and flowers for arrival. Status: check. I could add some chocolates, but from the photograph, it doesn't look like she eats at all. Taxi booked for pickup. Status: check. Cannot use my car, it smells too much like an ashtray. Outfit picked out. Status: check. Actually, not checked. Okay, then, check, but only after consulting Misha, Ric, the doorman, my bai, well, basically everyone who is unfortunate enough to know me.

I am all set. I am going to wear a pastel salwar kameez—harem pants and a tunic. One of those short, trendy tunics. They were probably also in vogue when Gucci Mama left for foreign shores, back in the days when Bollywood screen diva Asha Parekh was a style icon with her generous derrier.

All righty then, there is my answer: time to change the outfit.

Finally, I go in for the demure look. Misha comes over once again to drape me in my one decent sari. I think I am getting acclimatized to the idea of a mother-in-law. Why else would I be in a red sari!

I take a deep breath, calm my nerves, and give Misha a quick hug before stepping into the elevator. It's going up. That is a good sign, right? One elevator ride later, I find a jet-black Mercedes waiting to take me to the airport. I look at the smart driver suspiciously. "There's been a mistake. I asked for an Escada." I have visions of the hole in my pocket widening.

"No, madam, this is the right car. Escada not available today." Fine, if this is a complimentary upgrade, so be it. This has to be my lucky night.

The flight is scheduled to arrive at midnight. Karan said I didn't need to go, as long as I arranged for a safe taxi. These drivers are as safe as can be, not to mention dumb enough to send me a Mercedes in place of a budget car. But in consultation with Misha and Anushka, it was determined that I should not let go of this opportunity to make a stellar first impression. Therefore, here I am in my bridal red sari and black Mercedes, ready to dazzle.

I reach the airport with fifteen minutes to spare. I decide to wait in the mosquito-free confines of the car and disembark five minutes before the appointed time. I mentally rehash my conversation with Karan. He was concerned that I might not recognize his mother. I politely reminded him that I had seen her photograph. Actually, I had spent almost the entire evening with her photograph on the night of his party. Unless she's had another face-lift, I will be able to recognize her. Of course, I did not tell him that.

My watch says five minutes to midnight. It is time to rock and roll. I try the car door and it does not open. No problem, I will just try the other one. It doesn't comply either. The driver, true to his training, exited the car once we arrived. And true to his ilk, he strolled away at the most inappropriate time. I tap the tinted windows with my knuckles, then my hands, and finally my fist, all to no avail. I heard a soft click when the driver exited the car but was too busy contemplating the steps leading up to my grand encounter to pay attention. It was a fatal mistake. The car has one of those fancy central-locking systems that locks automatically after a stipulated time once the key is removed. I try my luck with the front door. I lean over to try the driver's side and step on my sari. There is a gut-wrenching rip. And, to make matters worse, I find both front doors locked. I ripped my sari for nothing! I try the car horn twice, but that evokes no response. There is no choice but to sit tight. My sari is torn beyond repair. When Mama Bhatia does her annual inventory of my expensive saris and jewelry, this piece will definitely need some accounting for. But I will worry about that later. First, I have to get out of this death trap!

I call the cab company and tell them of my predicament. Five minutes later I watch the driver running back to the car. He quickly opens the door to my irritated *"Kahan nikal gaye the aap!"*—Where had you taken off to? I know the answer, it is usually *beedi, gutka,* or *peshaab*—smoke, tobacco dip, or piss. This whole ordeal has cost me fifteen minutes and potentially a very eligible man.

The British Airways flight from London has come in fifteen minutes ahead of schedule and I am fifteen minutes late. Never mind, I trust the Indian immigration and customs department. It will take her at least forty-five minutes to complete the formalities.

Well, guess what? Things have changed and I'm not speaking of my luck. The customs officials are not as predictable as our neighborhood thullas. I am informed that the flight was cleared ten minutes earlier and that the Frankfurt flight is going through immigration. *Okay, calm down…* I have missed Gucci Mama. I feel much better after saying it out loud. People turn to look at a strange woman in a torn red sari speaking to herself. *No problem. Call the hotel and check if she has arrived.* I discover that she has not reached the hotel. Fine, she is on her way then. No problem.

This is when my imagination takes full flight. Here is a woman who has not been to India in twenty years and has never been to our worthy capital. And because of me, some depraved lout is probably navigating her along the loneliest stretch in the city. I start to perspire profusely in the cool night air. I am toast. What if she doesn't make it to the hotel? What if something happens to her? And, most important, what if she tells Karan? What if he breaks up with me

and marries Tantalizing Tanya? There is only one
way to find out.

"*Driverji, gaadi hotel le jao.*"

As we race to the hotel, I flash into the future of
the Verma household. I see Tantalizing Tanya in an
apron with Gucci Mama and Karan in this totally
domestic setting. They are having dinner or something at his house, with everyone sitting around ex-
changing pleasantries. And Gucci Mama says,
"Thank God you broke up with that girl, Karan.
Can you imagine, she nearly cost me my life!"

"I know, Mother, what a close shave that was,"
he replies apologetically.

"And the way she dresses . . . Even children were
scared of her," Tanya agrees, her hand massaging
Karan's arm. They all start laughing. . . .

"Madam, we have reached." The driver looks at
me with concern.

I come back to an even scarier reality. I unclench
my fists and get out of the car. We reached the hotel
in record time. I rush to Reception and discover that
Gucci Mama checked in twenty minutes ago and has
immediately requested a "Do Not Disturb." I can't
call on her. My misery is to last until the next day.

"Aisha, you look like a mess. What happened to
you?" It's Rajat looking me up and down in a hugely
condescending manner. Damn him!

"Just stepped on my sari while rushing here." I
do not meet his eyes.

"You really should be more careful about the way

you dress when you come to the hotel. It can give a very bad impression," he says in a professorial tone. Translation: The boss will hear about my disheveled appearance in the morning. I keep mum for fear of saying something incriminatory. Besides, I am afraid that if I open my mouth I will bite his head off. I turn to leave and hear him whispering something to one of his recent conquests at Reception.

I don't know what has got into me. But on the way home I call the car service to make a request. Posing as a VIP guest's secretary, I cancel his pickup from the airport. Mr. Schultz is a regular and a very fussy guest at the hotel. I am certain he will find our representative booth at the airport and get to the hotel. The person who will have a hard time is my colleague, Rajat. And, for once, things go as planned. Alfred Schultz "totally takes Rajat's happiness" that night. He vows to take the matter up with the general manager. I guess my disheveled appearance at the hotel gets put on the back burner.

I think about returning Karan's call that night, but it is past 1 A.M. And how am I to explain the mishap? Okay, confession time: He called when I was driving back from the airport, but I didn't take his call. What could I have possibly said? "Hi, Karan, I lost your mother. I think she's probably somewhere on this fog-induced highway with a psycho cabbie. But don't worry, it's only one in the morning!" Now that she is safe in her hotel room and resting, I am ready to speak with Karan, but only in the morning. I've had enough excitement for one day.

I have to be back at work at seven in the morning. That leaves me with fours hours of sleep. As it turns out, even four hours is way too much. I toss and turn through most of the night, trying to console myself with the thought that I took care of everything right down to the last detail. This is just plain sore luck. You can't explain these episodes or blame anyone. It's easier to make peace with the fact that the disaster has happened.

The next morning I am still racked with anxiety when I spot Gucci Mama heading for breakfast and hide behind a pillar. That's what stress does to you. She doesn't even know what I look like, and yet I duck. I am not above spying, however. I follow her to the restaurant and try to sneak a look at her, which isn't too difficult as she is surveying the buffet counter. There are two prunes and one smoked tomato on her plate. She has bypassed the croissants, blueberry muffins . . . everything worth eating, really.

I stand close enough to take in the details. Gucci Mama is beautifully put together in a light pink outfit with beautiful leather caged shoes to match. Her hair is carefully coiffed and she wears very little makeup. She doesn't need any. Her smooth skin shows no signs of aging. A double string of pearls caresses her neck. She is everything I imagined her to be—sophisticated and understated. And she scares the daylights out of me.

Karan calls at that opportune moment. I decide to take it. "Hi."

"Hi, Aisha, you had me worried. What happened to you last night?" I switched off my phone after his first call the previous night. Luckily, before I incriminate myself, Karan carries on. "Thanks for arranging everything." Is he being sarcastic? It's too early in the relationship to know for certain, and our recent history has been bumpy. "The car was waiting for my mother on arrival and the room is very comfortable. I tried to call you, but there was no response. I was just not comfortable with you going out there at night alone."

Which car was waiting? I am too old for fairy godmothers, but this isn't the time to be skeptical. I decide to play along. "Not a problem at all. Can I call you back, Karan? Something's come up."

"Sure. Anyway, call Mom soon. She's dying to meet you. And let's all go out for dinner tonight. I'm taking an early flight back."

"Sounds great!" I make a mental note to eat heartily before dinner. If I am going to have to eat steamed veggies, I will do so on a full stomach.

I quickly run back to my office to investigate. What happened was simple. A car was sent by default. I arranged a car from elsewhere but didn't inform the hotel, so they sent one anyway. I love this company. I am going to be working for them for a long time.

————

I am ready for Gucci Mama, no, for Karan's mother. I get to the locker room and realize that a sleepless night did not help the bags under my eyes, but on the other hand, my face does look thinner. I touch up my face and tidy up the sari and go back to my desk. I decide to leave a message for Gucci Mama in her room. It is better not to disturb her at breakfast. Besides, considering what she has on her plate, she will be done in a few minutes.

I sit down at my desk and look at the list of tasks for the day: ensuring that the welcome packages for an ongoing conference of neurologists are placed in their rooms before noon, going over the table setup for yet another wedding at the hotel, and then, of course, completing some boring old paperwork. I don't know when I got promoted to being the wedding planner, or maybe it is D.P.G.'s way of rubbing it in because weddings are definitely *not* my responsibility.

I put away the pile of papers and pick up the phone. The boss materializes just as I am about to call Gucci Mama. I am superstitious. I feel that when you are about to do something of supreme importance, you should not be *tokoed* or interrupted.

"Aisha, good morning. There's this training in the evening. I can't make it; you have to go in my place."

"But, sir . . ."

"Aisha, it's a whisky-tasting session. I'm sure you'll appreciate that. It starts at six P.M. Be there." And he strides off to his morning meeting. I vow to get back at him somehow. This is getting out of hand.

I decide to place the call to Gucci Mama anyway, but first I have to decide whether to call her "Aunty" or "Mrs. Verma." She is a guest at my hotel, but she is also Karan's mom. Will "Aunty" be too familiar? No. What would be familiar is "Mummyji."

She answers the telephone in one ring. "Good morning, Aunty. This is Aisha, Karan's friend. I just wanted to welcome you to the hotel—"

"Madam, this is Housekeeping. Guest is not in the room."

"Then why did you let me keep talking?" I snap. I hang up with the ugly frown that always makes its appearance when I am irritated.

"Excuse me," a gentle voice says.

I look up, frown in place, to find Gucci Mama standing in front of me.

Oh, shit! I'm wearing the ugly face! Damn. I quickly replace it with a gummy grin.

"Are you Aisha?" she says in the same sweet tone.

"Yes, I am." I smile, exposing some more gum.

"I am Karan's mother. I just wanted to thank you for everything."

"Please, it was my pleasure."

"I guess we will chat in the evening over dinner. Karan will be back by then. I don't want to bother you at work. I'm off to the spa for some indulgence. See you in the evening."

I actually like Gucci Mama. So she is Botoxed and stuff, but she doesn't have the brittleness that one associates with the most important "other" woman in a man's life. She is elegant and gracious. I have a feeling that we are going to get along just fine.

And then the boss butts in yet again. "Aisha, I have given in your name. Be sure you're there at six," he says while gliding past me. Is this man on Rollerblades or something? The only reason he's missing this opportunity for free booze is because it is at 6 P.M., the time he canoodles with his wife's sister. God help him if he isn't there when the Mrs. gets home.

Hic Hic Hurry

*I*t's 6:15 and I am sitting in the Raj Kamal banquet hall, which is strategically situated near the rear exit of the hotel. The whisky-tasting thing has not even begun. I am to meet Karan and his mother straight after work at 8:30. I am just about ready to walk out when people start streaming in. After a few preliminary introductions, we finally commence our journey through the undulating hills of Scotland with the wonderful taste of single-malt whisky.

I think you know you're drunk when your thought process glides from bagpipes to the men who play them, and then on to wondering what they wear under their kilts. The problem with one of these tasting sessions is that what begins as a harmless get-together with a few sips thrown in invariably becomes bingeing without your being aware of it.

I can do a great job of looking sober when I'm

not. Believe me, it's part of being a socialist, I mean socialite. That's an overstatement; it's part of being a wannabe. You have to hold your liquor while playing the jolly drunk. Besides, I am at work, though not technically. I am off the clock at 6 P.M., so my job is safe.

"Aisha, it's over. Move." We are squeezed between a wall and a never-ending table. Rajat is waiting for me to move so he can leave.

"It is?" I ask, slightly disappointed. All good things come to an end too soon.

I slide my ample bottom over six chairs and finally find an open space. I detest this kind of seating arrangement. How are people supposed to get out? My colleague has neatly glided off the other end and is enjoying a good laugh at my expense.

"Very sh-mart," I shout at no one in particular and slide across the row of chairs in the other direction. This stuff is good. I have a Scottish accent just like Sir Sean Connery's. Okay, I am slightly tipsy.

I look at my watch to discover that I have fifteen minutes to sober up. I retrieve the homeopathic Nux Vom from my bag and pop a few pills and wonder if one can OD on Nux Vom. And then the phone rings.

"Hello, beta, how are you?" It is Mama Bhatia. She has obviously recovered from our little tiff.

"Good, Ma. I'm in a hurry, can I call you later?"

"Why, what happened?"

"Nothing's happened, I'm just in a hurry."

"But you've finished work." The inquisition continues.

"Okay, I'm going out with this guy and his

mother tonight," I splutter and regret it almost instantly. Never talk to your mother when tipsy.

"Oh, beta! That is wonderful news! God bless Swami Raman. What are you wearing?"

"Later, Ma, really . . ."

"Okay, fine. All the best. Why didn't you tell me earlier? "

"Ma, can we talk about this later?" I interrupt the "all is forgiven once you wed" speech.

"Fine, but as soon as you get home, call me."

This impromptu confession is going to cost me big time. I go into the locker room and desperately try to make myself presentable. I am splashing cold water on my face when the phone rings again. I juggle the phone with one hand while trying to grab a towel with the other.

"Beta, a sari is most appropriate . . ."

"I'm going straight from work, Ma. I'm changing into jeans. And she's seen me in the work sari, so she knows how I look in it."

"That's not the point. It's important to project the right impression."

"I know, Ma. Next time. Okay, okay, bye."

I can't deal with her quite at this moment. I dab on some gentle exfoliating face wash and start to massage it into my skin. The phone rings once more.

"I hope you're wearing some jewelry, not your semiprecious stuff. The diamond jewelry."

"I don't have it with me here. It's at home," I answer, trying not to get foam on my phone.

"Beta, how many times do I have to tell you?

It gives a very khandaani impression, real solid jewelry, very familial. Listen to me. Let me call Lata, she will bring it to you at the hotel."

"Mother, stop it. It was a big mistake telling you. Please stay out of this. And I have to get ready now. So don't call me. I will call you."

"Fine, beta," my mother responds with a tone of resignation.

There is soap in my eyes now. This face-wash stuff is not as gentle as it claims to be—my eyes are bloodshot! The phone rings yet again.

"Please stop calling, I will call you!" I scream.

"Aisha, are you okay?" It is Karan.

"Oh, hi. Crank calls . . ."

"And you'll call him back? That's a novel way of dealing with it."

"Well, I know the caller. Anyway, what's up?" I keep my fingers crossed. Maybe he is about to cancel.

"Nothing, we're waiting in the lobby. Are you ready?" *Shit, shit!*

Never any luck! At least one thing in my life is constant.

"Can I meet you in the parking lot in ten minutes?"

My eyes are red. I am just a little tipsy, but I will be able to conceal that. My jeans are a little crushed, but I don't think anyone will notice in the dark. But my hair looks great. I am going to focus on the positives. I have a little twist in my walk, but only the expert eye will be able to tell. To anyone else, it will seem like I have a slight problem with heels. It's quite another matter that I am wearing flats tonight. But yeah, I am as ready as I will ever be.

I reach the parking lot in record time. I have to run a bit, but that's fine. As I take a gulp of air and slide into the backseat, my senses are assaulted by overpowering perfume. It isn't a bad fragrance, but I am beginning to feel queasy, and heady perfumes don't really help.

"Aisha, this is my mother. Mom, this is Aisha." Karan makes the introductions.

"Karan, we're ahead of you, we met this morning." Gucci Mama smiles pleasantly.

I present her with one of my best smiles and remember just in time that I have forgotten the mouth freshener. My breath smells of a brewery, but one from Scotland. I am no cheap drunk!

"We first pick up Natasha and then head to Italiano's. You remember meeting Natasha, don't you, Aisha?" Karan asks.

I recoil into the backseat. "Yes, of course." Great, uptight cousin Natasha is also going to grace the evening. If he had told me earlier, I would have worn my bulletproof vest!

We reach her a little too quickly and she jumps into the backseat with a cheery "Welcome, Maasi!" She is all joie de vivre. It's as if the French have coined the term for her. It lasts till she sees me cowering in the back. Yup, me, the ol' cog in the wheel; guess the Americans coined that one for me.

"Hello," she says tersely.

"You remember Aisha, don't you?" Karan asks.

"Of course." She smirks.

This is going to be a long evening. Luckily, familial bonding and the "What's happening to so and so" takes over.

My phone rings. Mama Bhatia just won't let go. I reject the call this time. My mother has a tendency to scream into the phone and I don't want the whole car to be privy to a conversation that will be entirely about them.

"Is it that caller again?" Karan asks with concern. "Aisha has been getting crank calls all day."

Natasha sort of humphs and raises her eyebrows, giving me a look that says "I know what you're all about and you can't fool me." Great, I can have a whole conversation with her eyebrows now.

What is it about being around a guy you like and his family? You end up second-guessing everything he says and that extends to his father, mother, cousin, and even his dog. I'm not exaggerating here. I love dogs, don't get me wrong, but not when my entire romantic future rests on the wagging of their tails. Have you ever dated a guy who's a dog lover? Suddenly, whether Bruno or Bosco wags his tail when he sees you is such a big deal to everyone!

"No, it was someone else." I slide back onto my mental roller coaster.

When we are all seated at the bar, Karan orders a bottle of Sula Satori. "The table will be ready in twenty minutes," the steward informs us. I politely decline the wine. That is how sick I am starting to feel. The puke is at the base of my neck; I look around the place in an attempt to distract myself.

"Bit dull for you, isn't it?" Natasha whispers softly to me.

I ignore that and focus on the overwhelming feeling of queasiness. I am not a whisky drinker. I desperately try to hold back the wave of nausea. My eyes soon begin to wander around the room as the conversation moves to Nicky Aunty. I am not trying to be rude, but I have to keep myself occupied to distract myself from the puky feeling.

I observe the tired look of the bored bartender. The staff at this place range from bored to dull. It must be the hiring profile. He is pretending to listen to a woman seated at the bar. A cigarette nestled between her manicured red fingernails catches my eye. I can so use one of those right now. Just then the lady does one of those barstool swivels, and her head comes into focus like that famous clip from the *Exorcist*. It is the boss's wife.

In all seriousness, I feel sorry for the woman. Here she is getting slammed, and the boss is nowhere in sight. It's sex at six for him, whereas she is a raving drunk by ten. And then she does another swivel and spots me.

"Aisha," she shouts, stumbling off the stool, and heads toward me.

There is nowhere to run, so I decide to surrender gracefully by slowly rising to offer her my cheek in humble obsequiousness. But the kiss lands straight on my nose, pseudo-Kiwi style. She immediately plonks herself down on the stool next to mine. I sort

of smile apologetically at my entourage and try to
make the introductions. But she is way ahead of me.
"Hi, cutie, we haven't met." The boss's wife is looking shamelessly at Karan.

He smiles in response. "Hi, I'm Karan, and this
is my mother and my cousin Natasha." He is totally
unfazed. *Gay men, pint-size divas, drunk and flirta-
tious women—all the same to him.*

"So is he the boyfriend? You clever girl." She
winks, giving me a hard nudge. I almost topple
Gucci Mama's vino. "That's okay, I'm sure Aisha
won't mind sharing. She has my man all day, don't
you, darling?" She gives me another aggressive
push. This time I lurch forward and nearly throw up.

"That's it!" Natasha stands up and flings her
napkin down in a grand gesture of self-righteous disgust. "Bhaiyya, you may think she's the perfect
woman, but she's nothing more than a tramp. She's
into all kinds of stuff . . . If Maasi wasn't here, I'd tell
you. She even tried to pick me up!"

Karan looks shocked. Luckily, Gucci Mama is so
Botoxed that her face remains expressionless. But I
can well imagine what she is thinking. Even the
hostess who is hovering around loses her bored look.
At least I discover that she does possess a range of facial expressions.

"So Aisha's a naughty girl . . . How interesting!"
the boss's wife slurs, totally getting into the conversation. I ignore her and look at Karan. He is all that
matters. I actually feel sorry for him as he looks at me
expectantly.

"Natasha is right. She met me with Anuj and I

was trying to set him up. I guess I felt bad and guilty about the whole car thing. She thought we were a couple and that we swing. But I was only doing him a favor. And this is my boss's wife, that's how we share a man."

Karan looks relieved and Gucci Mama bursts out laughing. But it is more than I can endure. The puke is tickling the back of my throat. I get up and run to the cloakroom. I lock myself in a cubicle. Leaning against its flimsy wall, I wipe the tears away. The phone rings once again.

"Hello, beta. How is everything? Anyway, don't talk too much. Be quiet and listen. Must not reveal too much, it could be used against you later...." I think we are way past that stage.

When I return, Natasha and Gucci Mama have left. Karan has found us a private corner table.

Karan sits me down and then slips into the chair next to me. "My mother was tired and so I sent Natasha and her home in a taxi. I'm sorry for putting you through this, I know you've been going through a rough time." He thinks I am still in love with the ex—this evening is just getting better and better.

"Where's my boss's wife?"

"Not to worry. I called for her driver and helped her into the car."

"Thanks. That was so embarrassing."

Then Karan is suddenly down on one knee and looking up at me with a silly grin on his face. I, for my part, am feeling the onset of a well-deserved anxiety attack. Hands clenched on my lap, I look at him half in expectation and half in fear—*what is to follow?* "Allow me a minute," he finally says.

I nod mutely, for once totally unsure about what to say.

Karan pulls out a scroll of paper from his back pocket and drops it with a flourish. "Are you, my fair maiden," he begins in a hilarious falsetto, " 'a young lady from an upper-middle-class family with strong traditional values, a postgraduate in literature, of fair complexion and modest demeanor'?" He pauses as I look on in shocked wonderment.

"Do you 'hail from Nashik, a small nuclear family of four, and—' "

"What is this?" I exclaim, making an attempt to grab the scroll from his fingers.

He dodges my hand and continues to read.

"Are you 'a humble young lady of generous proportions . . .' "

That's it! I stand up in complete embarrassment. He has got ahold of the profile Mama Bhatia loaded on the website!

"You think this is funny!" I fume.

I get up to leave, my face hot and flushed.

"Aisha, wait," Karan calls out to me.

I pause but refuse to turn around.

Karan gets up and places his hands on my shoulders, gently turning me around. "Aisha, I'm sorry, baby. It was a joke, a silly idiotic joke because I'm just too chicken to come out and say it. But here goes." He stops meaningfully and looks me straight in the eye. "Uh, well . . . what do you think of marriage?"

"In what context?"

"I don't know . . . In the context of Princess Di and Charles? Why does it have to be in context?"

"I think she shouldn't have married him. . . ."

"Hold on, I was being sarcastic. I mean, what are your personal views?"

"I don't have personal views. It's not like it's important, like world peace or global terrorism."

"So marriage is not important to you?"

"Of course, it's like on top recall nowadays. It's just that it's not as important as say . . . global terrorism."

"I was speaking of marriage and me and . . ."

"You, marriage, global terrorism . . . Interesting tangent."

"All right, Edward De Bono, let's ditch the lateral-thinking bit and save it for the business grads." Karan pulls me closer. "Let's play word association. Here we go . . . marriage, me?"

All that happens is that I experience a full-blown panic attack.

It must be a minute, but it seems like forever as we stand there looking at each other in silence. Finally he breaks the silence. "So will you?"

"I . . . I . . ." I begin inarticulately. "I don't know."

"You don't know?" he asks in surprise. "I've heard of people saying yes or no and sometimes maybe. But *I don't know*?"

"It's because . . . I really don't know, I mean I like you and all that . . ."

"All that?" he counters, his voice getting a little terse.

"I mean, I really like you and stuff, but this is un-expected, we weren't even speaking last week and now this?"

"Aisha, spare me, okay? Let it go, I'm not in the mood for a brushoff."

"Karan, I'm not brushing you off . . ."

He waves his hand as if to stop me from talking. I stop speaking for fear of saying the wrong thing, as I usually do.

And then, just like that, he leaves. I continue to stand there for a long time, thinking of nothing. For once, I don't have my usual dose of psychobabble to help rationalize my behavior.

Diminished Logical Thinking

Sometimes I feel that the desire to love outweighs the desire to be loved. That has to be the reason why so often we continue to love those who don't deserve to be loved. It helps us feel emotionally employed. *Amour* becomes a career, a vocation. So we continue to draw from our depleting inner reserves while steadily moving toward emotional bankruptcy. Why did I turn Karan down? What was I thinking? Did I not know how deliriously happy it would make my mother?

Predictably, the phone rings just then. *"Bacchi, tumhari ma hamare saath hain.* She is very worried about you."* A squeaky voice comes over the phone.

"Namaste, Swamiji," I whisper. I don't know if he heard me, for he continues with his ramblings. I guess godmen are prone to monologues even on the phone.

"*Ab chinta band karo.* The time has come." It's almost as if he is predicting an apocalypse. "*Samay ab theek chalega. Ab* relax *karo. Bahut aashirwaad, beta.*" I stare on in silence for a few moments.

These *Hinglish* godmen are a boon for our nation—thank God for their easy accessibility. They're like your neighborhood kirana seth, the mom-and-pop store owner who speaks the English of a department-store clerk and the Hindi of a *thelawala* who pulls his vegetable cart from neighborhood to neighborhood. A very comforting combination. Plus, of course, he stocks everything from Indian veggies to face bleach. And he does home delivery.

I get to work later that day and call Misha. She assumes that I am busy that evening and has excluded me from her plans. The worst thing about being in a relationship is the automatic assumptions your friends make. They assume that now that you have a man in your life, you will suddenly be incommunicado and discover a whole new set of priorities. The only people who genuinely appreciate the new addition to your life are your dinky friends. The husbands are particularly happy because for once there is someone to split dinner tabs with. It is not an urban legend: Men usually do pay for their wives' single gal pals.

"So, how are the preparations for the evening going?" I ask later that evening. Misha is off on one of those speed-dating nights. The American rapid search for love has finally caught on in India. I expect her to launch into a tale of how someone met her husband at one of these events. But not this time.

"Not going," Misha replies.

"What happened?"

"Remember Gurinder, my childhood friend who lives in Canada now? He is coming down to Delhi for a night. Anyway, I have to meet him today before he leaves for Bhatinda."

"You haven't met him in years. Do you *have* to meet him?"

"Bade Papa's orders." Bade Papa is Misha's father's older brother. He is the patriarch of the joint family and his word is law.

"Sounds fishy . . . It feels like a setup to me."

"Never. Aisha, he's a complete nerd!"

"Okay, so just take him to the speed-dating thingy."

"Please, and let all of Bhatinda know that this is what I'm up to! This guy is a pathetic wimp, I don't want to scandalize him."

"So what will you do?"

"I don't know . . . Go to dinner someplace where no one knows me and then drop him off at his hotel," Misha says, sounding quite sad.

"I'm sure the speed-dating thing will happen again some other time."

"Not till next January. I thought maybe I could meet someone for New Year's."

I know exactly what she is talking about. New Year's Eve is the most pathetic time to be single, apart from Karva Chauth and Valentine's Day.

Actually, I would even rate it above those two. Karva Chauth, although spreading rapidly, is a predominantly North Indian fetish, and Valentine's Day belongs to the younger generation. Therefore, escape is possible. However, on New Year's Eve, everyone, be he or she old or young, is out there celebrating. In all fairness, a New Year's Eve bash is great till about fifteen minutes before midnight. Then it gets insufferable as it deteriorates into the couples' version of a scavenger hunt, with everyone seeking their better— or rather missing and drunk—halves. And you sort of stand there as people push and shove you around, looking over your head, your shoulders, well, just looking through you for their special someone. Then the lights go out at midnight and you stand alone waiting out the couple of seconds that feel like hours.

The one time in the recent past when I was with a special someone on New Year's, we were stuck in traffic at midnight listening to Prasar Bharti while doing the countdown. All because the ex wanted to party hop in fog that was fifty feet thick! I didn't speak to him for a week after that. We split three months later. I still believe that fateful evening of the thirty-first had a lot to do with it. Think about it: *31* is *13* in reverse!

Misha's chances of finding a date for New Year's are thwarted by this old aquaintance making an appearance in her life. There is nothing much she can do about it. Bade Papa will not be put off. She dresses in an ultra-prim salwar kameez and leaves the cigarettes behind. She climbs into her stilettos, deciding that if God has not blessed him with a growth spurt, it is entirely Gurinder's problem. As she leaves her place that beautiful and breezy evening, Mrs. Mukherjee takes in her new look and gives her the thumbs-up.

Misha reaches the hotel at the agreed hour and calls for him. He promises to be down in fifteen minutes. Misha settles into a couch in the lobby. It is a good vantage point. Hopefully, her field of vision will cover all entrances. She sits back, missing her cigarettes, and wonders at how strange life can be. The last time she was at this hotel, she was executing the marital downfall of the adulterous Sharad. And here she is now, demurely attired and with feet crossed at the ankles, waiting downstairs as if to say she is too shareef, chaste, to see the insides of a hotel room with a man.

Misha is fortunately not one to waste time on self-analysis. She quickly switches tracks and starts using the time to make eyes at a cute gora—white man—on his laptop, while simultaneously waiting for every ugly guy to walk up to her. It's almost like playing Russian roulette. The appearance of every unattractive guy is like the spinning of the cylinder. And it keeps spinning as Misha waits for him to walk right up to her. As he passes, she releases a silent breath and waits for the next ugly guy to approach her. Suddenly, she feels a tap on her shoulder. Gurinder has closed in on her from behind.

She turns around expecting to see a pock-ridden face, but what she encounters are dimples paired with a set of twinkling eyes. The delicious mouth challenges her to accept the fact that he is gorgeous, and he has had more than just a growth spurt.

"Guru?" Misha can't believe her eyes.

"I believe that's me." With that brief exchange Misha finds herself sucked into a vortex of Yash Chopra movies—he's the king of Bollywood-style extravaganzas. Without warning, old visions of her running in fields of sarson to meet her lover merge into the updated slow-motion sprint in a field of daffodils with Guru—very Bollywood meets van Gogh. And just like that, everything changes.

Suddenly, the second oarsman has bailed out and I am left steering the raft alone.

Misha leaves for Bhatinda with Guru. I am not kidding. She leaves the very next day. They chatted all night long and decided that this was "it." Just like that, friendship blossomed into love and Misha is on her way to meet the family. Bade Papa and Co. are delighted with this development and a quickie roka has been arranged. All this in a span of just four short days! I still believe it was a setup, but it's worked.

Then Anushka calls me with her news. She is setting up a garment export business with the old friend she met again at Karan's party and is leaving for Italy.

"I'll be gone for a month. I'm really excited about this venture. I think I'm going to finally make a new life for myself."

"Anushka, are you sure? I mean, this is so sudden. What if it doesn't work out? What if you lose all your cash?"

"I don't know the answer to all those what-ifs, Aisha, but I've got to give myself a chance."

I take a long walk that evening—I, who take exception to any form of physical exercise. But I recall once hearing that there is nothing like a long walk to clear one's head.

So I take the long walk, and it does not help. My thoughts are riding this dizzying carousel, spinning around and around. I like the guy, I like his mother, I even like his shoes, why then don't I know whether he is the one? What will it take for me to realize that someone is the one? I know for a fact that Mama Bhatia has her little overnighter packed with her best Kanjivarams and is waiting for the go-ahead, but it is not to be, not this time anyway. Misha is engaged and getting married to someone she has met again after years. Ric and Nic are back together and are working their way around Mrs. Mukherjee's intrusive presence. Anushka is off to Italy. Everyone is taking his or her measured risks. And here I am, desperately holding on to the status quo, only because I don't know what I want and frankly never have!

Let's Get It Started

Misha calls me that night from Bhatinda and voices her steely determination. "I'm going to sleep with him."

"Congratulations, Mish."

"No, I'm serious. We have to do it. What if we're not compatible?"

"How does it matter? From what I've heard, married people don't have sex."

"That's just something single people say to make themselves feel better."

"Et tu, Brute?"

"No, this is serious. I think I have to do it."

"Do you want to, or have to?"

"Doesn't matter."

"Do you think he expects you to be a virgin?" I ask, finally getting to the point.

"I guess not. We haven't talked about it."

"Are you going to?"

"No, it's not important, I'm sure he's not."

"I guess . . ."

That night I lie in bed and replay my conversation with Misha. Sexual compatibility is important, but is it sufficient? These days, it's like the last bastion to be conquered before one travels down the aisle. A betrothal is a visa to a preconjugal tryst and most people are keen to make the trip, which makes me wonder just how many virgin brides there are in the world.

Anyhow, the question itself seems outdated and I try putting the thought out of my head as I toss and turn in bed. I have more important issues to deal with. I have lost the man I am in love with. I have not spoken to Karan since that night at the restaurant. And he hasn't called either. I need time to think . . . time to sort out my emotions. I lie in bed, trying to force myself to sleep.

My mother calls the next morning as I am getting dressed to go to work.

"Beta, how are you?"

"Just getting ready to go to work, Ma. I was thinking about coming home for a few days." I know cool single gals go to Goa or someplace like Singapore, but my bank balance tells an altogether different tale, one of a broke, albeit cool, single gal.

"Chalo, very good. I was just going to tell you to come home."

"Why?" I ask suspiciously.

"Mini is getting engaged, it's a good opportunity to meet some boys."

Shit, shit, shit!

"I have to see about the leave..." I try to back out.

"*Nahin beta,* I'm sure you can manage. It has been a year since you came home. Book a ticket with Lata and Sachin. Actually, I will let them know."

It gets better and better.

A few days later, I am on a train, all set for the twenty-two-hour journey to Nashik. D.P.G. has been very accommodating despite my insistence that if he needed me, I could easily postpone the trip. His disappointing response is a smug "I think we can manage, Aisha." *Damn him.*

Karan is away in Mumbai on work—again. I discover this by chance when Rishi has some of the belongings we'd been storing while he moved sent over to his place. He left without saying good-bye. If that isn't enough, Lata Didi jabbers nonstop about Mini's good fortune at having bagged a corporate hubby and how at twenty-four she is getting married at just the right age, blah blah...I sort of nod through the conversation with the well-rehearsed smile of a hotel professional. I am obviously going to do a lot of listening on this trip. The good news is that I am safely ensconced on the topmost berth and get away with the periodic "huhs."

Mini has just turned twenty-four. Her fiancé received an MBA from a university in California and is an investment banker. He is an only son. *So what! So what!* I lie on my side with my back to the world, turning myself over to slumber. In the distance I can hear Lata Didi's persistent "Aisha, Aisha...," but I choose to ignore her.

I wake up a good four hours later with a foul taste in my mouth. I carefully make my way down from the berth. It's heartening to see that dusk has fallen. I find Lata Didi seated with a petulant scowl and Jiju looking happy with a silly grin transfixed on his face.

"Jiju, can I have that Coke?" I spot the bottle lying on the table.

"No!" Lata-di shouts in typical Hindi film style.

I recoil at her reaction. This is way too dramatic even for me.

Jiju breaks in. "Let her, Lata, she is not a child." *Hello! It's only Coca-Cola.* "Go ahead, have some." Jiju winks and offers me the bottle. I take a sip and realize that it is too much whiskey and very little Coke. I swallow distastefully, not because I have an issue with drinking onboard a train, but whiskey and Coke is a definite assault on the senses. Jiju laughs at my visible discomfort. "Still a little girl, huh," he slurs and grabs the bottle from me.

Lata Didi squirms. I let out an awkward laugh and leave the compartment.

I stand unsteadily over the steel basin and rinse out my mouth and splash cold water over my face. I feel mildly refreshed as I lean against the wall by the open door and watch the trees whiz past. The night air caresses the droplets on my face.

I must have been there three minutes when Lata Didi finds me. "I'm sorry, Aisha." This is the first time in my whole life that I see the vulnerable and contrite side to my cousin. Normally I would savor the moment, but something in her manner restrains me. She stands by my side and continues. "Marriage is not all that it's cracked up to be. After a while, it's just two people living under the same roof. And you find yourself accepting things you never thought you could ... His drinking has progressively worsened." I observe her in surprise, but she looks straight ahead and continues speaking like she has never spoken about this before, and then it strikes me that she probably hasn't. "Now he drinks to get drunk. Every night is a battle. But what do I do? It's been over ten years now and I'm only a college graduate. Where can I go? Papa has also retired. Aisha, it's good you've waited. You have a job, a life, friends, an identity...." She then turns to look at me and says with quiet intensity, "You know something, you will never be lonely."

I am speechless. I want to tell her that loneliness is a state of mind, but that sounds superficial and banal even to my own ears.

It surprises me how Lata Didi knows me better than I know myself. I have not felt lonely in the longest time, that's true. I bemoan my single status with my friends, but that's just "habitual banter," a Greek chorus, more for entertainment than an honest expression of misery. I am not discontented or lonely—in fact, far from it. I also know I want a wedding, but am I ready for marriage?

———

A few hours later I find myself settled on a hard wooden bench in the middle of a dusty platform in Bhopal. So let's go back just a bit. After my little chat with Lata Didi, I climbed up to my berth and tossed and turned for a good part of the night. I had to do something. I couldn't afford to lose a man who had come to mean so much to me. Finally, I wrote a note for Lata Didi, slipped it under the empty Coke bottle, and got off the train at Bhopal.

It is five in the morning and dawn is breaking. I rise slowly and make my way out of the station, stepping over sleeping bodies. This may sound trite, but it strikes me then that romantic love is at the best of times a luxury. While most people worry about where to sleep, a confused few agonize over who to sleep with. I take a taxi to the airport and buy a seat on the first flight to Mumbai. The Celine Dion version of the song "I Drove All Night" keeps playing in my head as I fasten the seat belt and close my eyes, refusing to think about what I will do once I get to Mumbai.

I hail a cab at the airport and give the driver the address of Karan's hotel. I miss him by five minutes. He has left and no one at Reception knows when he is expected to return.

"Is the bar open?" I ask, not fancying the prospect of hanging around in the lobby.

"It only opens at eleven-thirty, ma'am," the man at Reception answers indifferently.

"Fine, I'll wait then. For Mr. Verma, I mean, not the bar."

What does it matter anyway? Why am I explaining myself to this guy? I settle into a couch in the lobby and contemplate turning on my mobile phone but then decide against it. My mother is probably going ballistic, and who can blame her? I decide to send Misha a quick message to let her know that I'm fine.

An hour later, tired of keeping watch, I make my way to the bar. It is eleven-thirty and time for some fortification. My nerves are crying for some tonic! I settle for a screwdriver. It has some orange juice in it, so it has to be somewhat healthy, right? Three screwdrivers later, I am at Reception, professing to be Karan's wife wanting to surprise him on our anniversary. The world loves a lover and I am soon led up to his room. This is so easy, why didn't I do it two hours before? The answer is simple: I wasn't buzzed two hours ago.

I look around his room and feel strangely proprietorial. This is my man and this is his stuff. A book lies by his bedside and neatly placed next to it is a pair of reading glasses. I didn't know he wears specs; he probably looks really cute with them on. I check myself and cease snooping around. It's time to begin Mission Love Confession. I unpack the one sexy negligée I own. You're wondering why I packed it in the first place? Don't ask me, it's just one of those time-honored essentials in the single-gal survival kit.

I open the bottle of wine in the minibar and hum my way into the foamy bathtub. I remember Karan mentioning that his boss is this tight-ass control freak and plans their itinerary to the minute. Poor Karan, here I am sipping wine and bubble-bathing while he is probably running from meeting to meeting with the precision of Big Ben. I giggle silently. Big Ben is the name Misha gave one of her particularly well-endowed amours, while poor Anuj was called Tiny Tim. I take one more sip from my glass of wine and pour the rest into the tub. Just how decadent is that!

A half hour later I turn on the shower and savor the powerful gush of water. I crane my neck to look at the showerhead; as I'd guessed, it is one of those new massage ones. I will definitely travel with Karan on business when we eventually get hitched. This is awesome. I wrap myself in the soft towel and gather my hair to one side. On impulse, I pick up a bottle of cologne from the vanity—Gucci for Men, it reads—and spray it lavishly on my neck and bare shoulders. I smile into the fogged-up mirror.

I am sort of between opening the second bottle of wine—it's meant to reclaim the bravado that the shower has washed away—and holding on to the towel when the door opens, silently and without preamble. It isn't Karan but some strange man, about fifty years old, potbellied, and in shock.

"Who are you?" he asks in complete and utter bewilderment.

"Who are you?" I retaliate, holding on tightly to my towel and the bottle of vino.

I am immobilized. Besides, where am I to run? He is blocking the only exit!

"This is my room . . . and while this is all very tempting, I'm married." He gives me a lascivious look.

"Good for you, and this is not your room, it belongs to my husband."

"Excuse me, Satish." And in walks my knight in a steel-gray suit, head bent over a stack of papers.

"Uh, hmm, Karan, I have a little situation here. . . ."

Karan looks up and exclaims, "Aisha?" It is sort of a question . . . no, more like a statement . . . perhaps even an accusation. I am not sure. But it isn't good and I am lost for words.

"You know her?" The man turns to Karan in surprise.

But Karan is silent and I am . . . practically naked! He snaps back to reality. "Yes, this is my girlfriend. Aisha, this is my boss."

I can't believe it! This is the first time my boyfriend has seen me nearly naked, and so has his boss! Why is he making introductions in the first place? Shouldn't he be shielding me with his broad frame, protecting my modesty or something?

"I thought she said it was her husband's room?" The man probes further.

"My *future* husband's." All the courage I possess is squeezed into that one poignant remark.

"Aisha—" Karan tries to interrupt.

"No, stop. No more word games. Karan, please, I know this sounds weird, but can we put off marrying for a bit and like really get to know each other?"

"Wow," the man whispers.

Karan rescues the wine from my hands and I quickly tuck the fold of my towel in—he then gently takes my hands in his. "Aisha, I can't claim to understand you, but I do love you."

"So we are together then? Together, because we love each other's company? Not because we're bound to do the right thing or what's expected?"

"Meaning?" he asks, looking really confused.

"What I'm trying to say is that I'm okay with being the oldest bride in India just as long as when I do get to be a bride it is to the right man."

"I think I can live with that." Karan smiles and runs a finger through my hair.

"But . . . can you live without the other women?" I ask hesitantly.

"What other women? It's been just you for quite a while now. Besides, it's hard to say no to a woman in a towel."

"Oops." I blush.

"Karan, I think maybe you need some time—I'll be in the lobby." The man walks away, but we are past caring.

"I love you, Aisha. I think I've known for a long time that we are right for each other."

"So you knew from the first time you saw me?" I ask hopefully, milking the situation for all it is worth.

"No, not the first time. The first time I saw you, you had toilet paper in your hand, remember?"

"Okay, say no more."

"And as much as I love this situation, I have to get back to work and get you out of my boss's room."

"I thought it was your room."

"Both rooms are reserved in my name."

"Oh."

"Yes. And let's get you into some clothes."

"Yes, but I need to shower."

"You look like you just did."

"I know, but I smell of your boss right now."

He looks surprised, but I wave it aside. I have to wash his boss's cologne off me—the thought is positively sacrilegious!

Acknowledgments

I must as always start by thanking my parents, for their unflinching support in letting me lead the life I want to. Without their understanding, it would have been quite impossible.

My best friends—Clark Daniel Thomas, James Alday, Joshua Campbell, and Ryan Vila, who are continents away, but always so close—life always seems a little bit incomplete without you being a knock away.

In a book about friendship how can I forget so many others who enriched my life with their friendship: Mandy Smallwood, Bryan Mays, Emily Cooper, Steve Iverson, Laura Wells, Kay Wisner, Karen Pruett, Billy Neal, Beufort, Robin, Gabe Moore, Jimmy Ridley and Leslie, and so many, many more.

My professors, Peter Lawler, Steve Meyers, Bob

Frank and Greg Garrison, who let me get away with way too much, especially the lost Indian Girl Routine. When I was never really lost! But then, I suspect you always knew that.

And finally the wonderful warmth of the people of Georgia; it truly is always on my mind.

Big thank-yous to my agent, Maria Carvainis, who with her amazing wisdom and experience, made a dream come true from continents away. And my editor, Caitlin Alexander, who loved Aisha and made friends with her so effortlessly.

My cousin, Sanjay Dabral, and his wife, Ruth, who really did more for me than anyone I have ever known.

Hem and Kailash Joshi for all those Californian winters and holidays. My uncle and aunt, Jitin Bajpai and Ruth Defries, thank you for all your support.

My dear friend, Vishesh Sharma, who I have not met for way too long, I hope that changes soon.

And finally the many places that I have called home in my very nomadic life and the many people I have met along the way, who are now family. This book is for you.

About the Author

Advaita Kala may be best described as rebellious (a result of the years spent at Welham Girls School), confused (after four years of a liberal arts education at Berry College, Georgia), and multifaceted (having held jobs that range from being a librarian to a teppanyaki chef). After calling three countries and numerous cities home, she has finally dropped anchor in New Delhi, where she works for *Time* magazine. *Almost Single* is her first novel. For more information about the author, log on to www.advaitakala.com.